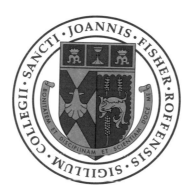

Lavery Library

St. John Fisher
College

Rochester, New York

by the Author

as Keith Botsford
The Mothers
Out of Nowehre
The Master Ruce
The Eight Best Dressed Man in the World
Benvenuto
The March-Man
Editors (with Saul Bellow)

as I I Magdalen
The Search for Anderson
Ana P

I I Magdalen

Lennie & Vance & Benji

(1998)

The Toby Press

First Edition 2002

The Toby Press *LLC*
www.tobypress.com

Copyright © II Magdalen, 2002

The right of Keith Botsford to be identified as the author of this work
has been asserted by him in accordance with the
Copyright, Designs *&* Patents Act 1988

ISBN 1 902881 46 X, *paperback original*

A CIP catalogue record for this title
is available from the British Library

Designed by Breton Jones, London

Cover illustration by Paul Desmond

Typeset in Garamond by Jerusalem Typesetting

Printed and bound in the United States by
Thomson-Shore Inc., Michigan

The Toby Crime Series

PREFACE

As Georges Simenon once remarked, all of us, brought to extremity by a sudden change in circumstance, can be compelled into a situation in which crime seems the only possible way out. Crime novels, then, are about such extremes of human behavior and they exist in all literatures. The French call them *noirs*; in Italy they are *gialli*; we used to call them "detective stories" or "mysteries", and most English and American ones have centered on the "puzzle" or "low life" aspect. But what has brought many remarkable novelists (Dostoyevsky, Balzac, Wilkie Collins, Graham Greene) to the genre is, I suspect, not so much the solution of a puzzle, but the fact that extremities clarify human dilemmas and afford the writer a clear narrative to follow. For a century-and-a-half readers everywhere have enjoyed them for those same reasons.

Whatever the type, all crime (or "espionage" novels from Buchan through Le Carré) novels rest to different degrees on action and character, and involve suspense. Suspense derives from not knowing how something will work out—hence the "thriller" which compels readers to turn the pages. But there is a substantial difference—it is a matter of the emphasis placed on character and language—between the least of these (many of which afford pleasure) and those which engage the reader at a higher level, whose pleasures are richer and more lasting.

Toby Crime proposes a series in which crime novels from many literatures are first novels and only then crime novels. That is, they are written for a literate public by writers who engage with language and society, and pose genuine human dilemmas. In that sense they go beyond crime to real life and real characters. The crime will not always be murder and they will come in all shapes and sizes, though the majority will be short. I like to think they would be enjoyed by Simenon, Greene and Chandler, as by Ian Rankin, Henning Mankell and Elmore Leonard among other contemporary masters of the genre.

KEITH BOTSFORD, General Editor

In most violent or unlawful events there is a perfect triangle: the doer, the agent, the victim. Each is as needy and dependent on the others, especially the victim. Even suicides follow the same pattern: the person on account of whom you did it, you with your feet off the ground, and the one who is going to cut you down, who is going to see you and smell you. You did it because you were unhappy? No, to make someone else feel guilty.

Igor Klíma,
Mental Trauma, *1988*

To Nina F.

Chapter one

His mother Mary Kay, that discarded rose, didn't know what to make of the boy. That was plain enough. Henning—good, trustworthy face, his long legs crossed—sat across from her, appreciating her slow, genteel voice, a winsome way about her, full of deportment lessons. He was charmed to be sure, meant to be, but what did it mean to say the boy was just her Benji, that's all? Didn't mean a damn thing, he thought, admiring Mary Kay's languishing neck, her beads, her soft hands. While her man, Craig—husband, whatever—wasn't around, she wanted to get in her word about her boy Benji, people here having been so rude, so unkind about him and her.

She was thirty-nine when she had him. "Twenty-two years after my first baby." She thought she was done with having kids, with raising them and watching them go off just like their fathers had gone before them. It hadn't worked out that way; she guessed it just wasn't meant to be.

"I'm sure you must have children of your own, Mr.... I've forgotten your name already, oh my!"

"Forsell," Henning said, thinking how you begin with the Mother-Son business, because that's the heartland. "But of course you love all your children, right or wrong. Whatever they do, whatever happens, they're still your kids."

Henning was a discreet man. He didn't say he had children, he didn't say he hadn't. He'd learned that the less you said, the more people talked to you, the better you can see them for whom and what they are. Henning listened, which was something he did very well. And she talked. Anyway, you couldn't get Mary Kay to stop going on about her boy, about what a good looker he had been for his age. She brought it up a dozen times in different ways until one wondered why, seeing as he wasn't around to enjoy his looks.

Fact is, Henning already knew a fair amount of the story and how people felt just by having been around Sapphire for a week or so. Two things helped. Born smack in the middle of the century, to the day, he was the right age. Not a whippersnapper or a smart-ass reporter. Luckily, he also had the kind of face—regular, unassuming, relaxed, on the heavy side, with hardly noticeable eyebrows—that people talked to. His many friends—all kinds of people in all sorts of places, cops, prison officers, attorneys, other historians, priests, money people, government people—might not know a whole lot about him, but they all said he was reassuring. Which didn't mean Henning thought he was, or that he was reassured himself, nor that he liked being middle-aged, whatever that meant.

It worked with Mary Kay too. She thought: this man from back East had been polite enough to write asking if he could see her (for Christ's sake who wrote letters these days?). Now she wanted him to know that being a good looker rated with her. "Looks and refinement", she was saying, "you only get from right breeding. Don't you agree, Mr...."

"Forsell, ma'am. Henning Forsell."

"They don't know a whole lot about that here."

Better believe it, thought Henning. A fool could see the woman was living in the remnants of plenty. Her looks had survived a lot better than her house. Judging from the light spots on the wall behind the mantelpiece, there had once been a lot more Ormolu clocks than there were now. Ormolu clocks and Biedermayer furniture from the old country. She'd been Mary Kay Rapp when she'd started out in life, and what was left of this farm in North Texas had been in her family, she said proudly, some time before Sapphire *was even* built a mile or so down the road, and had once been a whole lot bigger.

The boy, this graceful belated son of hers, was tall for thirteen, Mary Kay said, everyone said. He was a slender kid, fair, big-eyed, snub-nosed, and freckled. Very bright, too, his teachers told her. Only there wasn't a single picture of the boy. Not in her parlor at least. Her pride and joy? She just went on talking, as if she were reminiscing with an old friend. "Oh you know how teachers are," she said. "One will say, oh Benji's *so* mature for his age, so independent, and another one will say, he's still very young in some ways."

Henning had got the drift right away. Benji was anything but tough. By local standards, anyway.

"I guess you could say he was lonely, no one his own age around. Oh, I could just hug him to death," she said, dropping her voice and rocking her arms dramatically, as though someone were listening next door and she wanted her Benji to sleep, "though of course I wouldn't be allowed to do that...!"

Henning assumed she meant by that, because of Craig. Everyone Henning had talked to in town said Craig had some problems with his stepson.

But he was still her little Benji, more or less. Such are the fond illusions of parents, Henning knew: that kids are going to stay the way they started out. Had he been giving her trouble? He asked. They usually did, about that age.

"They do have minds of their own, I guess," Mary Kay said. "You can't control them the way you can when they're little. Oh, I know what people say..."

Pretty woman, Henning thought. What came off Mary Kay, like a faded scent, was gentility. Not just pretty, she'd even been beautiful, he thought: long, fair hair, blue eyes, delicate: as if she'd been sculpted out of light. If he imagined Mary Kay a girl still, guys lining up, Henning saw her family thinking no, this one's not good enough for her, that one's not her equal. She'd proven her family right, and they'd got less and less good, age being a slippery slope.

Benji must have taken after her. By all accounts he wasn't really like other kids in Sapphire, not like most of the boys in the Nava County Middle School where he went. Didn't make many friends. A loner. In parched places like Sapphire, Henning knew, that's what you said about any teenager who read books or wasn't quite like the rest, not so red-blooded.

Mary Kay explained how Benji might have been a mite lonely, the Rapp place being a mile from town.

"Your other children?"

"Oh, different as night and day. They've gone anyway. Never hear from them. I can tell you're a cultured person, that's what I thought Benji might become. If reading alone did it. Well, he just read and read. Shut up in his room. He'd read any book he could get his hands on, paid attention to the way he looked, was always clean and neat."

She was trying to say, Henning thought, that her boy wasn't a freak, a geek, a crazy, but for sure the boy who'd been her little darling, no longer did the same things he used to. He'd changed, which she guessed was normal, growing up as he was. "He was often, well, hostile, you know what I mean?"

She'd say, drink your milk, or have you got warm clothes to go out in, you know how cold the nights can get 'round here come fall. He didn't pay her any heed at all. He had his little blue canvas bag at his feet in the kitchen and his expression said, I don't live here and you're not my mother.

The handkerchief with which Mary Kay now dabbed a corner of her eye had a lace edge. It looked like it had long lain in a drawer and had been fetched out just for him, Henning thought. The handkerchief wasn't from here, and he expected her to follow its appearance up with a statement that 'round here people blew their noses on a paper towel.

For all the fuss she made over her kid, the bottom line was that the Kid's father was one of the men who had walked out on her. He given up teaching and was now selling cars in Dade County, Florida. Then another man turned up, and after him another. And then there was the present one, Craig. Small wonder, Henning reflected, that the Kid had resentments.

"Tell me about Benji's father."

She didn't have much to say. He was briefly present, a schoolteacher fresh out of Normal, doing the third grade for his practice year. Benji kind of looked like him. "People here didn't like Ben. He wasn't their kind."

"Benji's father?"

Any way you looked at it, Craig *wasn't* Benji's father, someone called Ben was. Why had they walked out?

"Oh it's all been so hard on Craig," she said. "He always did his best to be a decent Dad to the boy."

Only Craig didn't know where Italy was, which she'd always longed for, and he had never even looked at the framed pictures of Florence and Perugia that hung on the walls, old-fashioned photographs Benji had grown up staring at solemnly. However, as Mary Kay was saying, she didn't know where she'd be without Craig. She looked round her parlor shaking her head. "I don't know where everything's gone," she said, good at tears. Most everything had been sold off; Craig's wages kept a roof over their heads, and he looked after the place, fixed things, looked after what was left.

He'd noticed, coming in, how plum thickets flourished in what remained of the Rapp pastureland.

Mary Kay rose to get a little of her homemade cordial ("Why I've been neglecting you, Mr...."). A little nip made life a bit more bearable Don't you think, Mr...?") Restored, she added that Benji was no help with Craig's temper. "He'd never call Craig 'Dad'. He wouldn't even call him by his name."

She talked in scatters, but Henning was getting a clear picture from her. Of the boy standing in the kitchen and looking right past Craig when Craig tried talking to him. Past him or right through him. She was quite vivid.

5

Henning knew the Nava County Welfare people had been out this way. He'd sat in the one-day-a-week office they had in the bank building and talked about Benji with a black lady called Juweel with a powerful, oily presence. She had said, "If there'd been anything else as pure about Benji Dirksen as his hatred of Craig, he'd never have been in that mess."

The black lady used her words carefully. "Pure" hung in the air. It could mean so many things. Here it meant undiluted. Everything else might be mixed up about Benji, but not what he felt about Craig.

Generally, Henning kept as much distance as possible between his own sympathies and the terrible stories that interested him (this one was about as bad as it could be). He felt that was the only way he could be a medium for the people he wrote about. That was hardest to do with the victims, like Benji, who had less opportunity to speak for themselves—and most of them had none at all, because when he came across them they were dead. But he did feel a certain sympathy for Mary Kay, born Rapp, who was her own victim. A woman like her needed a man around this place, once one of the prettiest farms in the whole county, the only place with real flowers, with wisteria climbing up the porch and a proper vegetable garden: just like when she had grown up there.

Now Craig had come back to the house. Henning could hear him stamping his boots by the front door, then he showed up in the parlor door, barely nodding to Henning (Who the hell 's this guy?) and wanting to know if Mary Kay had any intention of making a man some coffee.

"Sure, Craig, I'll make some fresh, right now."

When the three of them sat in the kitchen, Henning saw that Craig wasn't going to talk about Benji at all. He just clammed up, and Henning wondered how long Craig had been around. Long enough, anyway, to bank up his fire at home, to lay clinkers and ash on his anger.

He had one of those over-elaborated fifty-year-old's bodies that have all their muscles in the wrong places: big forearms (he'd been a panel-beater in a body shop most of his life, and still was), soft, fat buttocks, a huge neck and florid skin. Looking at him, you could feel sorry for the Kid. Neither that, nor his being just plain hairy—the stuff, dark and wiry, spilling out his ears, the cuffs and neck of his sweat-shirt, over the belt on his belly—made him a bad man: just the dead opposite of young Benji. There were no fancy ideas in his head, no Italian landscapes, no art, no aspirations. The kind of man, Henning had been told, who said to his cronies, especially at the v f w Post (once Sapphire's one-room school-house), how sick tô death he was with the whole set-up. If his leg hadn't hurt—Viet Nam—and he could still go out and find himself a different job, make something of himself as he'd once hoped, he would have been gone long ago, getting rid of Mary Kay's "airs" and the kid's godawful superiority, who treated him like a hired hand.

The couple had had bad press: Craig because he could get violent when he drank, Mary Kay for being a lazy, inattentive, careless mother, putting her son at risk, letting him go work weekends in a hairdressing place with the two drifters who ran the place. Henning couldn't give her a specially good report himself, but he could understand how she might feel about her life dissolving, about her dreams of culture fading away, and about the once-upon-a-time (by all accounts) bonny, happy girl who was no longer either.

Well, Henning thought, a lot of people are like that. Things had gone wrong for him, too.

He watched Mary Kay hide her cordial when she heard Craig at the door. The antebellum drawl went and by the time they sat down in the kitchen she'd reverted to her everyday life, in which her function was to do whatever anyone around said she should.

Just about everything seemed to have contributed to Mary Kay's life-long defeat: her curls wouldn't hold in the heat; her eyes were washed out to a weak blue-gray and her glasses were dirty, which didn't help; her mouth, once so pretty, drooped; her children, except for Benji who was the last, were far away and almost never wrote; and Craig just hunted, and drank, and got into trouble—though he was known in town to be "crazy" about her, and that was the part she liked.

That wasn't enough?

Obviously not. When what happened, happened, Mary Kay hadn't been up to it. And Henning wasn't sure what kind of preparation could possibly have helped her.

On any Saturday morning a little more than a year back—say in July 1998—there stood Benji in the kitchen with his canvas carryall at his feet and his honeymoon with Lenny and Vance just starting. It would be around eight, and Benji wanted to get going. Mary Kay was absent-mindedly putting the milk back in the ice-box, Craig had just come in from some chore, and he'd seen the bag at the boy's feet, which reminded him that every weekend now, not doing what any normal kid would be doing, like playing ball with his Dad out back or helping out on the farm, such as it was, Benji was off to Sapphire, a mile away, to work for those two characters, those rats' asses, Lennie and Vance. Craig was the sort of man who didn't think that any normal boy would go work for a pair of hairdressers like Lennie and Vance.

Lennie (whom he'd seen several Fridays at the VFW Post) had at least been in the service, even if it was after Nam. But Vance, who sometimes came with Lennie, was allowed in because he was Lennie's guest and "performed" for the boys, he and the others sometimes called Nance—for queer. Making out that way he wasn't one himself, which was always a question.

"Just what the hell does the boy do at that there parlor?" Craig wanted to know. "He sweep the floor? We could use some of that 'round here. Plenty of work right here for those who don't think they're too good to do an honest day's work."

Benji had just looked out the kitchen window, as if the scrub oak outside had acorns. Craig could and did ask the same question, one way or another, every Saturday morning. He never got an answer. Neither from the boy nor from Mary Kay. The boy because he was an ungrateful, spoiled, sulky bitch, and Mary Kay because it was her job to keep the peace between the two people she shared *her* house with.

Mary Kay thought: if Benji didn't drink the milk that was his business. It was Saturday morning and he had to catch the bus in a quarter-hour: it only came by twice a day on weekends, and Craig wouldn't let her use the red pick-up, which was *his*. Then she thought, if he wanted help from the boy, or to know why he chose to work in town and save up money, why couldn't Craig ask the boy directly?

She thought that nice Mr. Forsell would understand why Craig wouldn't ask. He wouldn't ask because by then in Craig's eyes, the boy didn't *exist*. The boy might have been a dead body and you didn't talk to the dead, did you? And when she asked Benji what he had against his step-dad, he said: "You wouldn't understand."

The one thing clear was that since the end of the summer, every Friday afternoon when he came home from school, always neat, in regular shoes properly laced up, not sneakers, the straps on his book-bag done up, his eyes glistened with anticipation: because tomorrow was Saturday and he got to spend the weekend in town with Vance and Lennie. You could call that good, couldn't you? That Benji liked working? That he had get-up-and-go and took work seriously? That he was on time and saved the money he made from tips?

These two fellows from back East somewhere had started their hairdressing business about a year back, in what had once been the Knoblauch Livery Stable and then the town's first gas-pump. In places like Sapphire, she said, you liked to see the population go up by two, and having a hair salon was somehow civilizing.

Lennie was the nice one, the older one. The baby-faced one, Vance, she didn't like so much. Maybe there was something shifty about him. But Lennie, she told Henning, had sympathetic brown eyes. "You know anything about him, Mr. Forsell?" she'd asked. "I don't suppose you do, having been here such a short time. I just don't seem to understand how it ever got to be *like that* between them and Benji. I mean, these are people I know. I brought them good business. I had no idea…"

She wanted Henning to understand how Lennie and Vance had looked to her. She recalled that when Lennie first turned up he had a handsome, brief moustache, only then he'd cut it off. "It looked good on him," she said. "Not Hispanic, but like young lovers had

9

in the movies of the 'Forties. Land's sakes, Lennie did her hair once a month. She went to him rather than Vance because he was more solid. And because she didn't think Vance was respectful enough to the older ladies. For instance, Lennie never touched any part of your body except your hair. He was very careful and clean about things like that. Another good thing was, he never used dirty words or swore. Also, he liked musicals and even operettas, which he played in the shop, even the *Student Prince* that her father had liked so much.

And once Benji started working there (she went during the week, as Craig needed looking after on weekends), she always asked how her boy was doing in the shop. It wasn't that she didn't care or check up, the way people in town said.

Vance, who wasn't the one she asked, but the one who always did most of the talking and the joking in the Salon, said Benji *watched*. "He's some kid for details, he really learns, and he's got very gentle hands. You ought to try him yourself, Mary Kay, let him massage your scalp."

Her own son do that?

Hearing that, Lennie smiled, scissors in hand. "He's got a future," Lennie said. "He's got style. In the blood. Must come from you, Mary Kay."

"Oh, he don't listen to me one bit," she said, nonetheless pleased.

And Vance said, "Anything we do, he'll try. Ain't that right, Lennie?"

"Anything. No time at all, he'll be ready."

Henning understood all this was just talk. Salon-talk. Everyone talked while having their hair done. It was normal his mother should be pleased Benji was held in regard. And Henning was sure, had the boy been listening, his eyes would have glistened. The shop on Houston Street, the main drag in Sapphire, at the western end of which was the motel Henning stayed in, was a new world in which Benji felt he belonged.

It must have been an education. Lennie and Vance had been places. Not Europe maybe, but big cities like New York and

Washington. Mary Kay made it sound like they took Benji on out of the kindness of their hearts. She said, "They just kind of adopted Benji. I know he loves me still," Mary Kay said to me. "But he's moved on. Such a pretty, sweet child. And then suddenly he stopped being a child: after he started working in town. If I objected to something he wanted to do, he'd say, 'That's what adolescents do. Get used to it, Mom.' And if I didn't want him to have something, he said, 'I can buy it for myself.' Which was a shock for me, I can tell you. I didn't think they paid him, I thought he was just helping out and learning. 'Oh no,' Vance explained to me. 'We don't pay him ma'am, against the law at his age. We give him, you know, like presents. A share of the tips.'"

An education, but what kind of an education? Henning asked himself. His guess was that Benji had been agitated by the women who came in, by the details of their skin, the nails on their fingers which sometimes Vance did, the powder on their cheeks, the tiny curls on the napes of their necks. If his mind had fingers, they were going through the routines of beautification and learning the patter of the business. That was something Lenny and Vance had down cold, the flattery, the cajoling, the special treatment. They didn't offer just beauty, they sold rejuvenation: "There now Mrs. Herschel, you catch that bouquet at the wedding!" Laughter all around.

Vance was Benji's special friend. The boy, with basically just Craig to look up to as to what men were all about, would have agreed right away with Vance: that women were more re-fined: "Like your Mom."

In the shop, the three of them were all girls together. The ladies fell in love, Lennie was their Liberace. That much was the talk of the town, and Henning reckoned Benji had done more than just move on. He'd gone through the looking glass, and on the other side he'd become the kind of boy he thought he was. Not the kind they thought he was at home.

The glass of milk was an abomination. He stared at it as she put it in the door of the icebox and said, "I don't drink milk." His eyes were like milk, if iced, cold and clouded.

His stepfather took it badly: he bypassed the boy and said to his mother, "You going to let him sass his Mom like that?"

Henning reckoned Craig's agro was typical of the underlying coward, the kind who really wants to be loved. "Thinks of himself as one of the good guys," Henning had said to the Nava County Prosecutor, Ms. Pamela Baldwin, one night. "I'll bet all he beats up on is the helpless." Like hares streaking across the scrub, Mary Kay, niggers he had read about but hadn't seen. "The boy wasn't helpless," Henning argued, "so Craig had to ignore him. The one who got punished was his Mom, on account of her failing to make the boy into anything like the boys he knew and had grown up with."

"That's just a *supposition*," said Ms. Baldwin. She liked listening to Forsell, told people she found him "kind of neat", different. But she always reacted powerfully to the suggestion that there was anything more to her case than what met the eye. That was why she was such an implacable prosecutor: she was coolly certain of being right. Outside her office, saying goodbye, she rubbed her hands on her long linen skirt and said: "Mr. Forsell, you want to make out that the boy seduced *them*. I'm not going to buy that. That's ridiculous. He was thirteen, a kid in the seventh grade. What the hell did he know about seduction? And what would 'consenting' mean to a boy his age? People like you drive me nuts. You ask questions about the fucking *obvious*."

All that obvious, was it? The boy wouldn't drink his milk, he wouldn't look his step-father in the eye, his mother meant less than nothing to him compared to his new life, and nobody could keep him home weekends, make him do chores in the yard, drink beer or go hunting with Craig. The places in town where Benji shone were: the salon, where clearly Vance fancied him, and any place else he set his mind to being pleasing, such as school or church, where Pastor Samuelson, in whose choir Benji had sung since he was seven, said he'd always been a sweet, pliant child.

Henning's first judgment—he was still new in town and just beginning to see people who knew the Kid for the first time—was that if Benji was pliant, he was also a tease. He was different from other boys in Sapphire, and by rights, in a just world, he shouldn't have been growing up in such a place. Not at thirteen. Not with such parents. Not when Lennie and Vance arrived.

Chapter two

Once during their travels together, which took in a couple of years and, according to Lennie, twenty-six states, almost all of them flat and bare, crisscrossed by interstates, malls, motels and fast-food franchises, Vance said to Len as they were coming out of a ymca in Saint Louis, "Some pair we are!"

Sounds like nothing, thought Henning, but he liked to get under their skin, into their words, and the word "pair" made him uneasy. He'd sit in some diner or fast food place, usually with some local he recognized, buttonholing them, and nearly always he understood a little better how things were in Sapphire or any place else he went gathering up his material. It was his way, letting people talk, and he didn't think for a moment they were really a pair in the usual sense of the word. Maybe Vance thought so (which was his mistake), but not Lennie. You only had to look once at Lennie talking about Vance and you knew it wasn't so. What's more, when you heard Lennie out, you soon found out he was picky about words. Vance and Benji you might describe as a pair, that being the way most people in Sapphire grew to see them, but not Lennie and Vance. Because like Benji, Lennie thought, words were the bricks you built reality with. If you said you were a pair, that meant you were a pair, not that you'd like to be, might be, could be, or anything else. And in Len's eyes they weren't, and it was pathetic to think they were.

No, if Lennie Crace—smart son of Frank and Millicent, who were currently, he heard from Sheriff Overmayer, in San Jose, California—hung out with Vance, it was because Vance was of use. You told Vance to do such-and-such and he did. Go out and get me, did you bring back the paper, don't put ketchup on your steak.

But then Vance needed to be part of something, didn't he? A family, a pair, something. He wasn't much on his own. A hammer, a tool of any kind, is born to be used for a purpose. If the hammer never bangs a nail, is it still a hammer, or just a heavy piece of metal with a claw?

If you took Vance's point of view, that wasn't what Vance was thinking when he said what a pair they were. What he meant was that the things they did, they did together, and had been doing for two years before winding up in Sapphire. In school, Henning had known punks like Vance who had crushes on older guys like Vance had on Lennie. But Vance didn't have a crush. He went along with Lennie, with where Lennie was and what Lennie did, because it was obvious that he should do so. Lennie had the ideas; Lennie watched and listened. Indeed, Vance was quoted in their arrest report (before Vance's lawyer tried to lay the blame off on Lennie) as saying, "Some wives would dream of having a husband like Len." Meaning someone who observed everything, who spotted the slightest variation in mood or meaning, who was as attentive to the feelings and desires of others. Someone who could tell Vance in Saint Louis: "A pair isn't everything. There are matters on heaven and earth you've got no idea about. Like a pair and someone else. You have a cop on each arm hauling you off, that's a pair, and you're a third party. You find that exciting?"

"Two's company and three's a crowd."

Lennie had the sort of voice and language that would pass in most places for educated, which in fact he was. Vance envied that. He said that "when Lennie talks it just sounds serious, know what I mean?" And it was Lennie who told him there were "good threesomes and bad ones, just like there are good pairs and bad."

Vance had been alone for nine-tenths of his young life. Until he met Lennie when he came out of jail, nineteen then, being with someone else, anyone else, was what he'd always dreamt of.

When he said he'd been alone, what Vance meant was, alone in a crowd: in shelters, placed with families, in detention centers, in charity beds, in schools, in vocational training, in the kitchens he'd worked in, and even in prison. In all those places he'd felt people looking at him and thinking, now what the hell is *that*? Not who? What? The nuns, the first cops he ran into, a medley of welfare officers, casual strangers met in bars or men's rooms, the odd shrink he was sent to—none of them had come up with a real explanation. He was spectacularly queer and volatile, the kind of nasty little bitch you kept on a short rope. Henning had read all his prison reports. They didn't make good reading: snitching, blackmail, bum-buddying, attempted suicide, three doses of VD—these were just some of the things he was known for.

In a word, nothing in his nasty, brief, unilluminated life had, or possibly could have prepared Vance for the day Lennie brought Benji into the salon. He said: "What I thought was, a fucking angel had walked in. And Lennie was treating him like some urchin he had found on the street, you know, 'This here's Benji Rapp, he's interested in hairdressing.' That's *all*? I wanted to hold his hand and parade up and down the drag with him. I'd have killed anyone who looked at him the wrong way."

That was one of the early questions Henning faced. Did Lennie bring Benji into his Salon *for* Vance? That seemed likely, considering the tracks the pair had left, and how usually they went about their lives. Maybe seeing Benji that first time was the *fatal* meeting in Vance's life, as disastrous as first love. But it wasn't the decisive event. That had happened before, when Lennie picked up Vance. Lennie was to be *family*. He was to be what Vance knew. All that Vance knew. All that Vance had.

And it was, literally, a moment.

They'd both been sitting at the bar in a place called Pig Alley in Memphis, Tennessee. But not side by side. Some distance apart. Fresh out of jail, a bored, seated Vance was being chatted up by a lonely Master Sergeant who was both out of shape (which Vance didn't fancy) and a whiner (which he liked even less). Lennie, until that moment, with no one else near him, had been in conversation with Trish (that was on her nametag) about the country music on the TV overhead. Trish was cockeyed about him. About how he talked, the things he knew.

Then Vance reached into his back pocket for his wallet and put it down on the bar, halfway to where Trish was handing him his bill, preparatory to telling the Master Sergeant to go tell his sad story to some other sucker. The moment took place when Lennie suddenly put his hand on Vance's and the wallet under it, and said, "You're going to need that money where we're going, no point wasting it on an undistinguished clip joint."

Later, Vance told Jesus this must have been what He had in store for his little Vance. Medium tall, clothes tight on his body, low-slung, the way he liked men: more torso, less leg dark. Guys who emphasized how short Vance was, how his muscles didn't amount to much. Guys with an aura that other guys looked at. Lennie had that about him. He made space for himself, as if no one else belonged there. Also, the way he laid his hand on Vance's, right on top of Vance's beloved Rolex, was absolutely sure and firm. His talk, the way he used words. Hey, know anyone else who would have called Pig Alley "undistinguished"? Right away Vance felt he'd known the man all his life; and if he hadn't, he ought to have. He said to Jesus: It wasn't sex like You think. It was much more than that.

They got up from the bar together, each picking up his hold-all (Lennie's of genuine leather, Vance's of nylon), paid Trish, and Lennie led the way on foot outside. Didn't have a car, either of them. Didn't need a car, a car being something you took when you needed one, otherwise it was a nuisance and you had to think about it.

There was some sort of motorcade going on downtown, maybe a football team, but Vance couldn't see over the spectators' heads.

Where were they going? He forgot to ask and it didn't seem to matter. He just followed Lennie. Vance wondered when it would happen, and where. How did Lennie like it? Vance was more than willing to please, even if what they had together was a lot more than sex.

They walked some time—Lennie seemed to know where he was going—and fetched up at the Bus station downtown. Lennie chose a Greyhound bus heading South and paid for his own and Vance's ticket. When they climbed aboard, Lennie took a seat for himself and left it to Vance to find himself a seat way in back, where he had some sort of black preacher alongside. Vance liked preachers fine, but not black ones. But in back he had a window and could look out at the pine forests that took up miles and miles, the occasional mill or town.

When Vance began to feel sleepy, he did his hair with a pocket comb, something he did all the time, making sure he got the little wave over his forehead just right. Next he checked the pockets of his bomber jacket where he kept his most precious things, his Bible and the letters he'd got in prison that had, like the Bible said, invested his soul.

Then he went to sleep wondering how come Lennie was so sure who he was, and how he knew where he'd come from and what he'd been in for, that being the one snatch of conversation they'd had. Mostly Vance trying to figure out who this guy was. Which Lennie didn't say, then or ever.

Pig Alley was a known first stop for guys out of prison, the hold-alls were a sure-enough sign—but then Lennie had a hold-all, and Vance didn't know him from Adam the First Man. Maybe Tennessee correctional facilities left some sort of mark on you. It wasn't the prison pallor you saw on pimps and white-collar crooks in places further North, you spent too much time working in the sun for that. It had to be something else. Say the mark of the hard times a pretty young prisoner gets given on the inside, and all the things he had to do just to make sure he stayed alive. Maybe that was it. And why worry about it? Lennie knew what he was doing.

When Vance woke up it was the middle of the night, the bus

had stopped, and Lennie, carefully avoiding touching the plush seats and the feet sprawled in the aisle, made his way back to Vance and said they were getting off here.

"Where's here?" Vance asked.

Lennie said Greensboro.

They found a diner open a block away from the bus station, and Vance noticed how Lennie looked over everything and everyone in there, then how he talked to the fat lady who served them eggs and hash browns, talking her up so she gave them extra bacon for nothing.

When they'd finished and Lennie was fastidiously picking his teeth, Vance finally asked what had been on his mind during the long ride. "You're not the guy who wrote to me inside, are you?" he asked.

"You received letters, did you?" Lennie said coolly. "You carry on correspondences?"

"It is you, isn't it?"

Lennie wasn't into revelation. Not yet. So instead he said: "You want more coffee, or shall we remove ourselves?"

Vance started to giggle and Lennie said, "Don't giggle."

A hard one, Vance thought, but he stopped giggling and followed Lennie out of the diner.

A few blocks away they found a cheap hotel, the kind you see in black-and-white movies late at night. Cash up front. No questions asked.

Vance walked up the narrow stairs behind Lennie, watching the way his ass hardly moved. "Your room's at the end of the corridor," Lennie said, turning round and holding out the key. "It's all paid for, in case you're thinking of changing your mind."

"Why would I do that?" Vance replied with a smile. But Lennie didn't bother answering.

Lying alone in his narrow bed under a single sheet, the holdall containing all his belongings on the little table alongside the basin, Vance allowed that being alone in a narrow bed wasn't at all what he'd expected. But he'd met hard guys before now. It didn't bother Vance that Lennie could read his mind and knew that Vance wanted him. In fact that was all to the better. It was one thing to be hard, another to have a good clear head on your shoulders. So, if Lennie hadn't taken him right then and there, he had a good reason.

Having reached that conclusion, he got off his bed and on his knees and talked at some length with Jesus. Jesus knew him even better than Lennie. He knew how emotional Vance was: like when he giggled, which was just a sign that he was excited and flustered. He couldn't help it if he looked cute and guys came on to him. As usual when he talked to Jesus, the Lamb of God, Jesus prompted the answers to his questions and he felt immediately better. The question was: how had Lennie known who he was and where he'd been; and Jesus told him it was because of the way he walked. Vance knew all about that. Only his kind of people walked that way, their high thighs and butt a bit parted. He'd tried to do something about it but it hadn't worked. Whenever he was attracted to someone, that was the way his body responded.

Vance got into bed and passed his hands over his body, which was skinny and soft.

The last thought he had before falling asleep was: if Lennie had an eye for his kind, how come he was alone when he didn't want to be?

Jesus said it was what he deserved.

Though He hadn't done much for him, Jesus was Vance's constant companion. And his biggest secret. The only thing he was never to tell Lennie in the two years they were together was that he was scared of Jesus. Really scared. The nuns had done that to him. They had a way with details, those scary women in black. They'd told him why he ought to be scared. If He was crying on the cross it was because of what he, Vance, had personally done to Him by his many sins.

Chapter three

Henning said, if Vance "consented" to Lennie, maybe that was pretty much what Benji did, too?

Without answering his question, Pam Baldwin—she'd prosecuted the case—replied, "I'm curious about all this running about you're doing. They let you talk to those two, to Lennie and Vance?"

"Sure. Why not?"

"Why not? Because you've got nothing to do with the case. At least nothing you've said to me, and I've been pretty damn helpful, I think."

He saw Ms. Baldwin once or twice a week, never knowing if it was accidental that she turned up at Mary's Diner where he ate most days, or the times he went to Big Fork where the county had its offices, she somehow managed to bump into him in the court house, the public library or right out on the street. She was keeping an eye on him? She had some worries about the trial, which had been expeditious?

One thing he knew about her. She gave off a powerful whiff

of the modern girl she was—the kind that kisses the air alongside a man's cheek and thinks of him as just another guy, just like herself. At the same time, she was a big, tall girl, turning thirty Henning guessed, and he couldn't believe that somewhere inside the rigorous logic of her power suits and Neiman Marcus underwear there wasn't a large bundle of voluptuous thoughts.

There were times when she could be very abrupt and direct. As when she took another tack and asked him, still playing with the word "consent", "Do women consent to you?"

"Sometimes. Some women."

"Would you say they were right to do so?"

"If I'm what they want, I suppose so."

"Do they know what's involved? I mean, what they're getting into?" Henning said he didn't feel like being put on the stand that way. To which she said, "Get a life, Mr. Forsell. Relax. I'm just curious about how you've got the run of a case I handled going on a year ago. I think maybe I've underestimated you."

"No ma'am, you haven't. I guess you could say I have a number of friends in the business."

She gave him a half-smile, wiped a bit of cream that should have gone down with her Jello from her rich lips "And what business might that be?"

"Crime." He smiled back at her and then said, "And that's all you're going to get from me on personal matters… Ma'am. At least for now."

This time, her smile was more natural. "Okay," she said. "Later, then. I see you don't consent easily."

He allowed that was true; and thought, probably she didn't either. A fine-looking woman and she hadn't found a man? He said, "You want to know how Lennie and Vance became hairdressers? Buy you your coffee if you want to listen."

He moved over to a booth, ordered up coffee, and started telling her. It was stuff she could have known if she hadn't been in such a damn hurry. Stuff she ought to have known. Because there are always two or more sides to a question.

A police chief he knew in Tallahassee, Florida, had been one of the many cops he'd sent the word out to.

"You know police chiefs, huh?"

"Some."

"Who the hell *are* you, Mr. Forsell?"

"Knowing cops is my business. You want to hear, or you want to go on asking questions of a man who doesn't want to answer?"

There had been a complaint for credit card fraud laid against Vance in Florida, and it hadn't been reported by the man from whom it was stolen, but by a moving company paid with that stolen card. Because the moving company had been stiffed, and the girl who'd done the paperwork for the move remembered that two guys had come in, the smaller one paying, and she reported it to the police with a pretty good description. Two gays, one small, one tall. Anyway, how could you forget a move like that: after eight p.m. and the stuff to be moved being a whole hairdressing business: three chairs, mirrors, cash register, telephones, shelf after shelf of conditioners and dyes and stuff like that.

This particular caper was one of Lennie's impromptu ideas. The lads had been floating about for something like a year: doing "easy shit" and working their way up the elegance ladder—betters clothes, better apartments, a higher class of victims. Then Lennie said that what they needed was some sort of cover, and a respectable front. So they didn't have to shift from town to town, stolen car to stolen car, with no real time to relax and enjoy themselves. Furthermore, they needed some readies, a fair amount. Lennie thought the kind of petty theft that was Vance's specialty, was for the birds, and with Vance in tow, they couldn't do just anything.

Said Lennie: "Neither of us fancied dressing up in tutus and doing ballet, not window dressing, waiting in fancy restaurants— Vance could get pretty outrageous-looking some of the time—so hairdressing seemed like a natural. Queers all over, but respectable, because a lot of women are fag-hags at heart. The occasion, the opportunity, that was pure chance."

They arrived in Tallahassee, Vance and Lennie got their hair done just about every day in a different Salon, the kind that do big hair for the girls and have Tuesday afternoon discounts for ladies-over-sixty. Lennie would walk in with Vance and say, could they do a couple of guys. Most said yes. Then they'd sit down and get dyed or curled or cut and restyled, "just like a pair of high-class swishes," Vance said, who found it a lot of fun, and who anyway liked mirrors a whole lot.

They wouldn't look untoward as hairdressers, Lennie said. "The take is good and the suckers numerous. They may be just women," he added, "but they're married, most of them, to the respectable. And you never know what you can get from the respectable." What they had to do was learn the business and acquire the tools of the trade, which cost a hell of a lot—something like fifty grand, not counting the outgoings on a lease and the products.

It was not in Tallahassee, but in a small town some forty miles away, that the opportunity popped up. They were on the way back from a weekend in Georgia. A bad weekend. "Lennie," Henning explained to Ms. Baldwin, "was one of those men who can go all day without taking a leak. Nor does he seem to have any real desire for sex, of any kind, for weeks at a time. Not Vance. Vance gets stir crazy if he has to do without his kicks for more than a day or two."

What happened was that Vance had been forced to abandon their stolen car in a public park where he'd insisted on cruising. He'd picked this guy up, the guy had changed his mind, and there'd been an altercation, in which the guy hit his head on a rock. Vance had just finished dragging him behind a clump of bushes when a prowl car came cruising by. They had to get out fast. So from Georgia they'd had to hitch on a truck, and the truck had left them off at a Burger King where, right there in the parking lot, Vance had to turn the trick that constituted their fare while Lennie went inside and ordered up a proper breakfast.

This was on a Sunday morning.

At a booth in the corner, sitting alone and as far away as possible from anyone else, sat a plump, squeamish (he seemed to dislike touching anything on the plastic plate before him) forty-year-old.

Lennie picked him out. He didn't have a suntan, lacked cowboy boots and a straw hat, and wore shorts like a scoutmaster. His pink socks were held up by garters, his hair was combed in flat streaks to hide his baldness, and he held his breakfast biscuit with his pinkie out as though the biscuit were a cup of tea. Also, he was only pretending to read the paper propped up before him. Much of the time he kept looking up at Vance, who was as usual smoothing down the little coif of blond hair that was his "look"—derived from some long ago boy singer, maybe Frankie Avalon.

The victim's name was Michael Donnellan; he was in fact closer to fifty than forty; he was married and had two girls, both at college, both going steady, both apples of his baffled, unsteady eye. With that baggage and his hard-ass wife Heidi, the sixth daughter of a black Irish contractor, Donnellan should have known better, at least been more cautious.

"Well, he was cautious," Henning said. "He just didn't see this one coming. No record in Tallahassee, nobody under-age, cruising exclusively on Sunday mornings while Heidi thought he was off with the National Guard. Then he has a piece of bad luck. He fell for Vance like a ton of bricks. He was a natural victim, the kind of man Vance always went for. It was with people like Donnellan, maybe like Benji, that he got a chance to play the man, to lie on top when he was done."

It took no more from Lennie than a nod of the head for Vance to turn around at their table and smile at Donnellan.

Donnellan had a big old Buick outside, but he was reluctant for Lennie to come along, even "just for the ride." But then Vance told him a sad story about their having had to ditch a car in Georgia. But things were still awkward when the three of them—for the time being not a pair—walked out into the sunshine and asphalt together: Donnellan first, Vance next, and Lennie last, unconcerned.

Right up to the point of getting into the car, Donnellan remained uneasy. In the middle of the lot he turned around again and mumbled something about, "I don't know, I mean, your friend. I don't want any trouble…"

The lot smelled of fumes; back up against a chain-link fence was a dumpster spilling out polystyrene and paper cups with plastic tops.

"You don't have to worry," said Vance. "He's cool."

Vance was in the "state" Lennie knew well. When he was excited, it showed: his jeans shrank and the tank-top tightened over his indented and perfectly hairless chest, he fidgeted with his hands and when he walked forced himself to hold them tight against his sides.

"I don't know…" said Donnellan, still furtively studying Lance, his jeaned cool, the empty clarity of his eyes, and Vance, his hair-do, his short body. Donnellan's mind had to be racing, trying to figure out what this particular escapade might cost him. No, he didn't think Vance was an amateur. Not the way he returned his looks.

Finally Donnellan took out the car keys. Bad vibes made his hand shake, and as he bent over to put the key in the door, Vance's hand on his butt made Vance seem far away but all-powerful. "This is Lennie," said Vance. "He'll just ride with us, O.K.? It's your choice."

Though of course it really wasn't. Donnellan looked back, figuring this Lennie wanted to shake his hand or something. Nothing like that.

Vance was a persuasive liar, the kind who never overstepped the bounds of his imagination. The nuns had made sure of that. They made a big fuss with Vance about the truth, and all Vance had learned from them was that the truth got in the way of what a body wanted. Lennie was right: you could only be successful if you chose your victims with care. You picked out people who wanted to hear what you had to say, who chose to believe what you made yourself out to be. Willing people. Complicit people. That was the way Donnellan felt about Vance and mostly the way he felt on these Sunday outings: knowing something bad might happen, but letting himself be sweet-talked into it.

For Vance, it was all a scenario. He knew perfectly well what was going to happen with Donnellan. At least, how it would begin, the early stages. He'd been through the same drill many times now, ever since meeting Lennie in Pig Alley. If Lennie *wanted* something, it would happen, and in Vance's mind these preliminaries, the initial shock to his own body—what you might call desire—were all but over. You didn't have to be a genius to know that Donnellan wouldn't refuse, that he couldn't refuse, and therefore that what followed, followed.

"As for Lennie," Henning explained, "he was always detached. *Before*. It was like living in a place where the sun always shone and there were no seasons. There was never anything unexpected in these encounters of theirs. Nothing could go wrong. He had a lifetime's experience with victims, and it was reassuring to have one at his side. Who could be a more perfect victim than Vance? Vance's hand hadn't moved under his that day they met; it had just got warmer, as though it were blushing. Vance *wanted* someone to tell him what to do."

After a bit of shuffling about with his car keys and wiping his damp hands with a handkerchief, Donnellan seemed to realize that it was too late to do anything about Lennie; if you took on Vance, or anyone like him, you took your risks. It had been working for years' of Sundays: anonymous men in anonymous places. Out from Tallahassee to all kinds of suburbs and beyond, a different place, preferably a different county, each time. If you wanted to lose yourself, you had to do it where no one knew you. And even if sometimes it didn't work out (no one fancied him, the john of the day turned out to be weird, someone came crashing into the toilet stall or shone a bright light in the woods at the wrong moment), there were no real consequences beyond a little ordinary roughing up. The cops might haul you off to some local sheriff, you'd pay the fine for soliciting for immoral purposes, and that would be that.

All of this Lennie knew too. The problems started, for ordinary poor queers, when they didn't want to live the lives they'd set out on, when they acted straight and thought bent. "The way Lennie got round it," Henning said, "was not to touch anyone and not to let anyone touch him."

So Donnellan got in the car. Lennie sat in back on a seat covered in plastic, which he carefully wiped off first, and the three of them took off. The ride wasn't long, but Vance was amused by the way Donnellan studied Lennie in his rear-view mirror. How could anyone not trust Lennie? He looked so absolutely straight; he was so well dressed, so neat, clean, and shorthaired, his speech was so educated. Never did Lennie insist. He never raised his voice.

Thinking that was Donnellan's mistake, as acting and looking straight was Lennie's trump card. Always had been.

Donnellan chose the motel as if he knew it from before. While he was in the office paying for their room (cash, under the name Cary), Vance swaggered impatiently up and down by the Coke machine. By then Vance was fit to burst.

When Donnellan came out of the office, Lennie, leaning against the Buick's front fender, observed his ungainly butt as it waddled its way towards its fate; noted Donnellan's shorts were creased and his shirt had a large patch of sweat in back. Then Lennie noticed a last hesitation as Donnellan fumbled with the key to their room, a last look back at Vance behind him before he pushed the door open. Vance's hands were in the small of his back and pushed him in violently. Once the door slammed behind them there was no time left for hesitation.

It never surprised Lennie that people of Donnellan's sort, or Vance's, fell into their adventures without ever considering possible consequences. For instance that the car registration wrapped around the steering column and now in Lennie's hand, might show his name and home address, or that a batch of business cards in the glove compartment might show that Donnellan owned a salon in the state capital called "Hair Today".

A coincidence? Hardly. "Hair Today" was one of the places they'd had their hair done, and Lennie had checked it out since. Just as he'd checked out which highway to take from Georgia back to Florida and made the call to Donnellan, as if he were Vance. "Want some fun?" he'd said.

Consequences were Lennie's province, one that he ruled with considerable exactitude. No act was ever entirely gratuitous, and in their heedlessness people like Vance and Donnellan were, he thought, much like children. Sure of their desires, needy of their gratification, but totally unaware that around them were people, like himself, who thought out the next moves they would make long before they even knew they were thinking of making them.

Lennie was patient. From the back seat he continued to watch their room, to *see* it as though he were there himself. The TV at an angle up on the wall. Vance would have put it on loud. That way, if Donnellan cried out, whether in pain or pleasure—as if the two could be readily distinguished—no one would hear. The door to the shower ajar, the plastic mattress-cover on which Donnellan crouched, and the chenille bedspread and sheets pulled off onto the floor.

When he thought the moment had come, Lennie relieved himself, and then resumed watching, shading his eyes against the sun and the wavering asphalt of the parking lot.

They came out an hour later, Donnellan first. There was a welt on his temple and his plump legs, down to those terrible pink socks, were unsteady. Vance followed him out with a cigarette in this mouth. As usual on these occasions, his face was entirely expressionless; he was voided of all feeling or perception, and Lennie knew better than to talk to him.

Donnellan slumped down with his back to the brick wall. Effing woman! He was almost crying. Lennie got out of the Buick and walked over for a Coke, and while he drank it, his legs crossed, feeling good, he continued to watch. The hairdresser was trying to pull himself together. Well, thought Lennie, it wasn't the end of the world, was it? His first thought was that there would be other Sunday mornings for the likes of Donnellan; his second, that there could be much more fun for Vance.

Slowly, the hairdresser reassembled his body, slowly pushing it up the wall. This was going to be the fun part for himself, Lennie now thought, putting another three quarters in the machine: letting Donnellan know it wasn't over yet.

Of course the man had his dignity to think about. He stood up, looked at his watch, and found a pair of sunglasses he could put on. Seeing Vance standing by the Buick put him off momentarily, then he did what most people do when they know they've been really dumb and people are watching to see what they'll do: he began to make small talk—to Vance, who was too far away to hear him and too far gone to care—, to rub his hands, to saunter over to the car as though really nothing had happened.

Good boy, Lennie said, smiling, now make as if you're really master of the situation.

Then it was Lennie's turn to join the other two at the car, because Donnellan was reaching for the handle on the driver's side. Donnellan saw him coming and attempted a dumb smile. "Well," he said, "where can I take you fellows?"

For some reason, that really irritated Lennie. Again, it was the sheer heedlessness of what the hairdresser was saying. What was all this good cheer shit? People like Donnellan should have some respect. If Vance had any real manly guts in him, good cheer like Donnellan's, all that pretending, was the sort of thing that could get you killed instead of reamed? Not that there was much difference between the two, because in both cases you were had, you became a nothing.

For the time being, Donnellan was *spared*. He should be grateful and shut up. "It's not where you'll take us," said Lennie, walking right past him and getting into the driver's seat. "It's where we'll take you. Home, is it?"

Standing awkwardly outside while Lennie had his hand out to shut the door, Donnellan tried to smile. "Not home, no…"

"You've got a home, don't you? You don't like home?"

"My wife…"

Lennie had known all along he was one of those. "And your children, your reputation and all the rest of that stuff. I get it. She doesn't know you go cruising on Sunday morning when you should be in church."

"Sundays I'm at the National Guard. That's where I am."

Lennie liked the way his voice wavered. How could you be a man after that's been done to you? "Yes? You were in the war?"

"Let's get out of here," said Vance. "I'm hungry."

"I'm conducting business," Lennie said with ice in his voice. He turned back to Donnellan. "You were saying…?"

"I signed on for the Reserves."

"Only you don't show up. That's cool. So where do you want to go?"

"What do you guys want?" Donnellan said, beginning to break down again. "Money? Here, you can have all I've got."

"I asked where you wanted to go. You've got an office, somewhere you work?" Of course Lennie knew the answers, but the point was to reduce Donnellan to obedient jelly. In fact, it was a pleasure for Lennie to read Donnellan's mind, to know the hairdresser was asking himself how he had ever got into such a mess and promising that he never would again. Even more fun was to see Donnellan realize that if he gave away where he lived or worked, he might never hear the end of this; to observe the first shivers of fear in the man; to feel it sink into Donnellan that he'd always known that one day his habit would catch up with him. "At work, then," Lennie said as he swung off Interstate and drove straight to "Hair Today."

"There you have it," Henning said, "That's how they got to be hairdressers. They took even his cheesy name, Hair Today, right? Hair today and gone tomorrow."

"They're psychopaths," Pam said. "How can anyone want to dip into their lives?"

"I don't know about psychopaths. Seriously sick, yes. But there are no doctors for this sort of sickness. There's a whole, moist, terrible world under the one you and I live in. A sharp girl like you is not going to be surprised by that."

"I'm always being surprised."

"Must be because they teach you in law school these days to put the world right."

Why ask? That's what the Law was for, she argued. To keep life and places safe, to keep that other world—, where horrible things happened, where things that one couldn't imagine oneself doing were done—at arm's length. She said she'd never be happy as a defense lawyer. Hers was the clean job. You classify people like Lennie and Benji as inhuman, aberrant. You kill or shut up the people who did such things. Make the world right.

Henning said, "What's the use of it if you can't work out the pathology? Give you a couple of questions, ma'am. You think queers just naturally go in for this? That it's inherent in the way they have to live, on the margins? Are 'they' born that way? Or, are all children innocent?"

For the next three months they squeezed Donnellan out of his equipment, his lease, the cash he had in his bank, his car. All perfectly legally. He signed all the papers without protest. He might as well have been a circus elephant, kept in chains, abused, carted from place to place, and performing in public: still dressing hair, being allowed home to see his wife or greet his daughters when they came home for weekends, to barbecue in his backyard. But all the time his keeper was there, and *owned* him, became his partner, worked in his salon, was sent off to Vance in the middle of the day, or whenever, just to remind Donnellan that so far he'd been spared.

Ms. Baldwin said, "He's nuts to have let himself be blackmailed like that."

"You think Donnellan *liked* it? A dozen times he said he wasn't going back to his salon, he was going to move away. He couldn't figure out how he would explain anything to his Heidi, or to the two girls he worshiped. He knew what he was doing was vile. He thought it was vile. To be hurt and humiliated and turned into nothing; and if he thought that, what would his family think? Would you walk into the police station and tell the guy at the desk exactly what was being done to you, day after day?"

Donnellan thought about it, but everything told him that if the truth came out it would be much worse than it was with Lennie or Vance. What he had to do was last these guys out, cook the books when he could, keep the business going and shut up.

One Friday afternoon, he tried to scare Lennie and Vance away. He crossed the street from his salon and exchanged a few words with a cop in a squad car. Words about nothing at all. But he knew Lennie was watching him.

That night they didn't let him go home. Lennie told Vance to call Donnellan's wife and tell her he wouldn't be back for the weekend, that he was off on some exercise. "Say you're Corporal so-and-so and Mike here asked you to call. Tell her he'll be back Monday."

They kept him tied up and gagged in their motel room. Lennie hired the moving company. They were three states away when they shoved him out of his car. "When it was parked," Henning said. "Lennie doesn't like the hard stuff. Never really hurt anyone."

While Ms. Baldwin chewed on that, adjusting her bra, staring morosely into her third cup of coffee, wondering why just talking about these two made her feel sick, Henning said he thought Donnellan had got a pretty good deal. Definitely worth it to him. He lost plenty, but not what he had feared most to lose with those two: his safety, his life. That was why he never reported the loss or claimed his insurance. Heidi wouldn't have understood, his baby girls, his pride and joy, would have said "Yekh!" and fled, his father-in-law would have chased him out of town.

By then Ms. Baldwin had worked things out in her mind. She walked over to the counter and helped herself to a slice of cherry pie. "Hmm," she said, coming back, chewing, her little white teeth showing. "You don't think that hurts? Or maybe, Mr. Forsell, you think this Donnellan deserved what happened to him."

"Losing five chairs, two gross of shampoo, a cash register, that sort of stuff, that doesn't hurt half as much as the truth would have."

"So, how'd he make a living afterwards? How did he explain what had happened?"

"Cashed in his life insurance, went back to work."

"And just forgot about it? Didn't tell his wife?"

"Uh-uh, didn't *forget* about it. Just didn't tell anyone."

"And your delightful pair?" asked Ms. Baldwin.

"Not mine."

"Okay, Vance and Lennie."

"It was nothing to them. Routine. That's the sort of thing they did. It's hard to wrap your mind around the idea of people who live outside any kind of order, people who don't give a damn what anyone thinks of them."

Ms. Baldwin considered that, too. Then she said, "I swear to God, Mr. Forsell, you think I'm just naive, don't you. I wasn't all that well brought up, you know. I've got some street smarts, too, and those smarts tell me these guys didn't get even a fraction of what they deserved. They want putting down."

"People like Lennie and Vance don't belong anywhere in the scheme of things. I mean, people who do something just because an opportunity presents itself at the same time they *want* something."

"Shoot, you're not one of those 'It's-all-the-fault-of-my-Mom' sort, are you? You don't look like one."

"No? What do I look like?"

"Let's put it this way, you're the first guy I've met with a morbid interest who doesn't look morbid. Apart from that, I can't make you out."

Henning wanted to say—it was his method generally, the heart of the way he worked—that if you want to know what makes people tick, the first thing you need is patience. Whether they're crooks or women. How many "affairs" had Pam Baldwin been through in her thirty-something years, and none of them had worked out? Maybe she was in too much of a hurry.

He told her about Vance's nightmares: "You see, Vance tells everything to Jesus."

Vance not only talked to Jesus, he must have bored the hell out of Him, especially about how he'd tried to like girls, and what went wrong. The first one had been a thin tall girl who worked for Welfare. She had black hair, which she'd obviously cut herself, and looked like a boy except for some really tiny tits that turned him on. He'd jumped her by surprise and she'd just laughed at him. The second one was in foster home: a fat, retarded girl called Jacqueline. He'd more or less got in, only she squeezed him out of her, flabby and wet, as one would toothpaste from a tube, and then burst into tears, so that he had to beat her until she shut up.

The caseworker who told Henning about that one said nobody should be kind to Vance. He was a little swine. Everyone knew Jacqueline had a mental age of seven, if that.

"I'm telling you all this," Henning said to Ms. Baldwin, "on account of the way you and everyone else around here seems to want the case to go away. Crime's a black hole and things disappear into it, faster and faster. But it's there, even when you can't see it, when it represents a subtraction, when something that was no longer is. That's why I do what I do. You'll just have to believe me when I tell you I've been there and know what it's about."

"Oh shit," Ms. Baldwin said. "You're just a freak."

"No ma'am..."

"Can't you even use my name?"

"Okay Pam, if it makes you feel any better. Here's my thought so far and why I tell you about Michael Donnellan and Vance's sex life and how I'm going to go on finding out. It's that they came out here, Lennie and Vance, with the idea of soft living, not getting into trouble. They didn't consider Benji a crime. He was kicks."

Then he told her about Vance and Jesus.

"You know what Lennie told me? He said that he knew all along that if anything went wrong, it would be because Vance would do something incredibly stupid while talking to Jesus." Lennie had his eye on him, and though Vance never talked about Jesus to Lennie, Lennie knew all about his going off to church, the long talks he had with Jesus. "All the time, Vance had to know if Jesus was going to forgive him or if Jesus was going to punish him. He was so full of sweet Jesus that he had gone to church for months and had never even seen Benji singing in the choir. Lennie followed him one Sunday, leaning up against the back, and saw Benji straight off."

And when Vance came out of church and saw Lennie talking to Pastor Samuelson, Lennie left off talking and took Vance by the arm, saying, "Surely you don't think you can keep secrets from me?"

Chapter four

Lennie hadn't picked the Texas Panhandle or Sapphire. They happened across it, zigzagging West every month or couple of weeks on two-lane blacktops, and to Lennie, Sapphire just felt "right". The right size, clean, orderly, moderately prosperous, and, he felt after a two-day stopover, inhabited (Population: 1332, the sign said) by serious people who would mind their own business if you minded yours.

Henning, who came from an Oklahoma small town that wasn't all that different, felt the same way. He was always more comfortable off the phony coasts—New York and Boston, L.A. and San Francisco—in what he called the "real" America. He liked the people he met when he got to Sapphire: liked Sheriff Overmayer, a very still man; liked the go-getter Homer Jacquette of the Nava County Bank; he liked Miss Spencer, who had been Benji's teacher in seventh grade and Mrs. Alice Brougham who had him for the eighth; liked Maggie of the eponymous café where he ate and liked Pastor Samuelson, the black worry-bead who ministered at the First Church of Christ, belonging to no particular sect.

Henning came two years after Lennie and Vance, and he was

just fine there. So had Lennie and Vance been when they raised the local population to 1334. The doctors who'd examined Lennie both concluded that Lennie was probably cyclical, and was coming down from one of his highs, the cycles probably being how and why he got on drugs in the first place.

Lennie himself said that when he got to Sapphire it was with a strong sense of wanting to belong, something he'd not had since he was a kid.

Henning had some problems accepting that. First, there was the presence of Vance—if Lennie wanted to "fit in", why bring Vance along, who never would? Second, many of the people Henning had frequented in his travels, the people he studied, suffered from the same kind of nostalgia that seemed to bug Lennie, nostalgia for a distant small-town past, a place in which they had grown up pretty much like the inhabitants of Sapphire, a sort of paradise lost. With Lennie, could you take that at face value?

It certainly wasn't easy to get a fix on Lennie. Almost nothing about his past had come up at the trial, and even talking to him about his early days was a slippery business. All Henning knew, when he started out, was that Lennie was an only child. From his talk, it would seem he had a mother and a father who loved him. He had teachers, neighbors—a life. Then things had started to go wrong, and he'd never been able to recreate that life once it was gone. "I mean," he said once, "I don't feel that different."

Henning often felt a similar tug. He felt he'd had a happy childhood. Then things had gone wrong for him, too.

But his predominant feeling on arriving in Sapphire was that America was a fortunate place, and that the best of it lay in these sorts of places, places that were neither towns nor villages, but more like settlements that "just growed" and spent a long time acquiring their specific character.

Sapphire had flat land arranged in strips of brown, green, and black, miles of fencing, a jumble of cottonwoods down by the banks of the Upper Trinity, the bleached spires of silos, a main street with sober brick buildings and a bare white church in need of paint.

He could have inventoried it before he ever saw it: a Dairy
Queen, two gas stations and a garage, a bank, a post office, a motel at
either end of town, an elementary and a middle school (where Benji
was in his first year), a low brick building that housed the town's
"professionals", a veterinarian, a lawyer, and optician, a Volunteer fire
station, a VFW Post, three bars, Maggie's Café, a used car lot, the
football field (with metal bleachers and, behind it, a sort of half gulch
in which a few Mexican families kept to themselves), and what had
once been a railway halt, the long trains still occasionally rumbling
through, usually at night—eastward bound, clickety-click, westward
straining against the grade.

For a few weeks Lennie and Vance had stayed at the Tam
O'Shanter Motel on the west side of town. Vance was told to keep
himself quiet in his room and not get into trouble, but by week
two, Lennie, hanging round the baseball diamond in Rapp Park,
got himself invited to join the volunteer fireman's softball team: by
all reports he had an arm like a whip and was quick on the bases.
Homer Jacquette, the town banker, was the catcher. By the time fall
came round, Lennie had volunteered his services as auctioneer for the
Ladies' Auxiliary annual fund-raiser, and sold things nobody wanted
at prices no one could believe.

What people said about Lennie's early days in town, Henning
summed up as: smart, educated, didn't go to church, and though not
exactly distant, not the kind of man you had much physical contact
with. No high-fives, hugs, or slaps on the back. The ladies noted the
way he had with hair and themselves: respectful, coaxing, distant. If
he wasn't working, when Hair Today wasn't busy, he tilted back on a
busted wooden chair outside under his awning or, at lunchtime, or
early and late, just walked up and down, talking to folks.

What did he talk about? After scratching their heads a bit, they
said that apart from the weather and local gossip, nothing in particular.
Or at least, if you talked to him and then to someone else he'd talked
to, what Lennie said—about just where and when he'd gone to college or what he did there, about an early marriage that had ended in
tragedy, about his military service, almost wholly on Guam, where he

41

had been a medic—was kind of confusing. No one said to Henning that Lennie lied, just that things weren't always clear.

That more or less fitted the picture Henning was building up. In his experience, really good liars don't tell blatant lies, they hold back on the whole truth. It was his guess that Lennie maybe didn't really want to know the whole truth. It was like, if you are fishing, the way your line goes into the water at one angle, and in the water the line continues at another angle.

Chances are, Henning Forsell gave exactly the same impression, except he was more settled, more mature. The word was, he was real friendly, but you couldn't get personal with him. As to what he was doing in Sapphire, the only explanation he ever gave was curiosity. That he was, curious. He seemed to live in the slightest details.

Once, when Sheriff Overmayer came straight out with it and asked what the hell was so interesting about a pair of lowlifes like Lennie and Vance, Henning replied that of all the categories in society, criminals were the least explicable. "The extremes are available to even the most ordinary men and women," he said. "An extreme need be no more than the obsessive ticking of a clock. *Anyone* can commit a crime, which is no more than doing something wrong that most of us can't imagine ourselves doing. Why do they do it? That's of interest to society. If criminals could be explained, criminals could live among us as the sick, the old, and the daft do, about whom we know what afflicts them, and we can give it a name."

Pam Baldwin got closer than most. It was to her that Henning said that Lennie and Vance and Benji were perfectly ordinary people, made of the same stuff he and she were made of.

"And I treated them that way," she said. "The way the Law dictates for human beings, who have rights and responsibilities. We're not talking about a natural disaster here."

He said, "Take a look at these lists that Lennie made. Did you read his notebooks?" He shoved a thick bunch of Xeroxes across to her at Maggie's. "This one's a list of Michael Donnellan's assets."

She wanted to say, so what? It seemed to be the sort of boring list an accountant might make. But to Henning it was a picture. He could see Donnellan sweating alongside Lennie and helping him make the list. Henning said, "You're not interested in why fat Michael was so eager to supply information, to be so extremely precise? It doesn't remind you of the early Russian revolutionaries confessing to the most improbable offenses when on trial? To the radios they used to contact the enemy, the conversations they had with foreign "agents"? You've not run into that before? The need to confess? To make yourself out worse than you are?"

And then there was Lennie's mother, to whom—or so Vance said—he wrote once a week. All sorts of things neither prosecution nor defense had bothered with. "Apparently Lennie still writes her weekly," Henning said. "But no letters come back. Who knows if he ever even sent them. What do you think of that?"

"His father came when the trial began. But he didn't stay."

"They say the only mail Lennie gets is fan-mail, the usual girls proposing marriage."

Later, after Ms. Baldwin got back into her car and drove off, still unable to work Henning out, he went back to his motel room and dug out the transcript of Lennie's psychiatric examination, in which there were many—truthful…pity-seeking…? Henning couldn't decide—glimpses into Lennie's childhood absorptions.

"Leonard? Leonard! Where are you?" his mother cries out the back door. She keeps calling him, even now. The five-year-old Lennie feels his feet sweat in his sneakers. He is deep in the brush on the edge of the wood. The wood climbs up behind him, getting thicker the higher it goes. "Leonard? I know you're out there."

He sweats and gets excited. He would like to come out and tell her where he is, but he isn't quite sure where he is. "Leonard? It's time for church."

If he answers and goes back into the house, then whatever is about to happen won't happen, because he won't have seen it.

This happens often: when he's hiding in the garden, particularly at the edge of the wood; when he's in class staring out the window; later when he watches people more generally.

"What were these things that were happening?" the psychiatrist had asked him.

"Nothing special," Lennie had answered. "What some animal is doing to another, a cat catching a bird and playing with it. That sort of thing. I see a movie in my head. I know what's going to happen next. There's a warrior standing over a defenseless woman, he's about to lift off her scalp and hair."

Like Henning, the psychiatrist had read Lennie's notebooks, which had been entered in evidence. They were full of clues. For instance, that the things he "saw" excited him; they gave him a pleasant feeling.

In another, Lennie had seen a husband and wife coming out of a movie and he had noticed an "imbalance" in power between them.

In a third, a boy in his ninth grade class had been punished in front of the whole class because he'd spilled ink on Mr. West's desk. Mr. West was more powerful, so he could beat the boy. Lennie's function was to observe: as the boy cried in humiliation more than pain, as the bird flapped a broken wing helplessly, and the paleface woman looked up at the blade glistening in the brave's hand.

This last one, the punished boy, watching him crying with humiliation, was listed as Lennie's first sexual experience. He had come in his pants. Then and later, until he began to watch with a purpose, there had been nothing he could do about it. He wore two pairs of underpants and stuffed a handkerchief down his jeans. It hadn't embarrassed him. On the other hand it hadn't been something he felt he could ask anyone else about, to see if it happened to them, too.

Sometimes, not always, his mother called out for him and it happened. Now he made things happen which would yield the same result.

The next day, Henning found Ms. Baldwin lunching at

Maggie's again. Sitting down with her at the counter, he said: "You knew Lennie was married to a girl called Hope, didn't you? It's in the trial transcript and she was listed as his next-of-kin." He took out his notebook and read from it. "They got married on December 28, 1978, when he was seventeen. He was about to go to University. She was nineteen."

"You ever think about anything else?" she asked.

"Well, you're here aren't you?"

Ms. Baldwin was distracted. She had been holding a cigarette in her hand for some three minutes and hadn't lit it yet. "I don't come here to go back over Vance and Lennie. I come because I can't figure you out, and that bothers me. I don't even know how old you are."

"Born on New Year's Eve in '50, a minute before midnight. As for the wife, didn't everyone take it for granted Lennie was queer?"

"Sure. So he was married once. I'm sorry for the poor girl, whoever she was. But it doesn't change anything."

"She's been dead twenty years," Henning said quietly. "I don't reckon she needs pity. Or maybe you just have a kind of general pity for those who die young. Anyway, you won't be seeing me for a week or two. I'm off to Montana tomorrow. That's where they met. Then I'm going to Davenport, Iowa, which is where she died."

"You're a shit, Henning."

"And you really ought to light that cigarette of yours."

She did, and he thought it would be okay to have a dalliance with someone like Pam Baldwin, because he didn't think it would ever mean anything.

A few days in Montana gave him a clear enough picture. Between the two of them, Lennie and Hope, they had no more morals than plankton. Two of a kind, puzzled, disturbed children of the Prairie in dissolute times. They were artful, clean, and far from stupid. Both were travelers, both were well remembered. Hope more than Lennie. Local people didn't mind talking about the dead. They had established reputations. The dead weren't around to say, "No, that's not the way I was." And most of Henning's life had been concerned with the dead. Usually that was where he started.

This one, Hope, was gone, swept off a levee when she had no business driving there, on a motorbike at night during a storm, with the river raging and racing alongside her. Gone but remembered as an exceedingly pretty girl: on the delicate side in looks, and with a fondness for pretty clothes, perfumes, straight whiskey, and sex with strangers, sometimes for money. Maybe because she was an orphan brought up by Mormon missionaries and she wasn't made for the Coming.

From what Henning gathered, she did the rounds of the county fairs, the cattlemen's round-ups, the occasional medical convention, the more frequent revivals (at which there were always some ready to lapse). More than once, when he brought up what he thought Lennie might have been like twenty years back, someone would say, "No, she was the restless one."

The way people saw them, and it was long ago, it was Lennie who had just followed her around. One said, "He was a college boy." As if that explained everything. Another said—she'd actually rented them a small apartment she had over her garage—the impression she had of Lennie was that he'd left whatever he'd been behind him: "As if he'd walked out on his folks and wherever he came from, somewhere out West I think he said, Washington maybe, and was just drifting, looking for trouble."

If that was what Lennie was doing, then Hope suited his purpose. She had the experience. He didn't. He pursued her from encounter to encounter, from state to state, sitting, underage, in the same bars where she dickered for her price and what was included, or waiting for her among the cracked leather sofas and spittoons in the lobbies of commercial hotels, working their way slowly South.

Several times she'd said, "Get lost, kid."

That had had no effect. By the time they reached Davenport, Iowa, and Henning did, he'd worked it out that Hope was probably Lennie's first natural victim. Hope's mother (once or twice a year Hope went home, which was in Sioux City, Iowa, to rest up) was bitter about her. And about Lennie: "Hope told me all about him. She didn't have to have that kind of life, Mr. Forsell," she said, using a word Henning hadn't thought she'd say out loud ("She didn't have to be a *whore*").

Lennie *participated* (if that was the right word) in her life: in his own way, obviously, hands in his trouser pockets. It was possible she eventually fell in love with him, too. A handsome boy, persistent, admiring, with a sly and modest smile. And why not? In a life in which buyer (anyone) and vendor (Hope) exchanged very few words, what Lennie could offer was talk: and a desire to see what would happen to her. Or maybe, by the time they reached Davenport, she'd had enough of his eternal vigilance, of his dreadful patience, of his hanging around and watching, of the questions he asked her.

She didn't have to lead that kind of life? Marrying Lennie was supposed to straighten her out? Henning asked Hope's mother—there didn't seem to be a Hope's father anywhere around the house, not a picture, nothing—if she'd gone up for the wedding in Bozeman. "You must be kidding," she answered, "I didn't go up there, he didn't come down here."

"Your only daughter?"

"His folks weren't there," Hope's mother snapped. "…if he had any folks. Why should I be there? All I ever heard about his family was Hope saying he used to write his Ma once a week, that's all."

"She write back?"

"How would I know? They were married two months, something like that, then Hope took off."

"Why?"

"What kind of a man doesn't actually *do* it with her? Hope told me everything, I told you. Hope had to be passed out before he'd even come close to her or touch her."

"That would be with drinks?"

"Drink or drugs. Hope had a drinking problem, but she didn't do drugs before that boy showed up."

Not hard stuff, the police in Davenport confirmed, courteously looking back in their records. Lennie had a canvas bag full of different kinds of prescription drugs, uppers, downers, muscle-relaxants, anesthetics; straight from the pharmacy stuff, Henning read in the report of what was left in their motel room. And not a label on any of them. In the file there was also a report about being called in once by the motel manager. The maid had found Hope Crace tied down to her bed with tape and her face in a pillow. Had she tied herself, was there someone else doing Lennie's rough work? Whatever, making someone else helpless was Lennie's trademark all right.

Yet this was the man, Henning thought, who had no record at all, not a single arrest. *Nada*. And Hope was a Habitual. No fewer than eleven arrests for prostitution or indecent behavior.

What did that mean? It meant Lennie led a perfectly private life, devoted to his private pleasures, the taking of which apparently (that's the history of pleasure) demanded more and more.

Then the night she died, as opposed to all the time she'd invested in dying before that, Lennie wasn't there.

One report of her death in the local papers had it that she'd been doing the rounds of bars that night telling all and sundry exactly what Lennie did (watch her through holes in the wall, through windows, from a hiding place behind the bathroom door), and what he didn't do, *couldn't* do, not normally, only like a schoolboy,—jacking off (the paper said "masturbation".)

A barman in one of the last places she'd been, told the reporter he'd told her to watch out on her bike with the rain.

While in Iowa, Henning called all six Craces in San Jose, California, where Lennie's parents were supposed to be. On the last call he found a woman who said she'd taken over her apartment six months ago, and Mr. Crace had gone back to Washington *someplace*. He'd left a forwarding address. It was care of a lawyer. Henning called, but he wasn't in the office.

Dead ends and disasters you hear about twenty years late, Henning thought.

When he next saw Pam Baldwin, she made it plain she thought he was wasting his time with Lennie's past. "Those two were the sort of people who should never have been allowed in Sapphire or anyplace else. I don't know what you're after. You want to prove I didn't do my job, that Benji…"

"I haven't said anything about Benji."

"I know what you're thinking."

What was he thinking? He was reflecting on the nature of sexual pleasure. And was it pleasure that Lennie sought, or power? "You know what I'm thinking? About the fear of God; about shame? About what keeps us more or less within bounds? Remember what Vance said? 'It's *fun.*' Well, he didn't recognize any reality but his own. Nor did Lennie. Maybe we should ask, is sex harmless fun?"

Pam said she took two or three showers a day during the trial: as if that could wash away the stench. "They were animals."

Imagining her in the shower, Henning said, "Animals satisfy their appetites without much thought. There's not much ingenuity to what they do. My guess is, Lennie would say he's simply more advanced than we are. It could be that Vance is more normal: at least he couples with his own kind. Also, he talks to Jesus. By the way, which one of them did your hair? Lennie or Vance?"

She went all pink. "I never, Jesus, Henning, there are bounds, you know. You shouldn't overstep them."

"Sorry. Nothing personal. I just meant that something puzzles me. Lennie has instincts. For victims. But wouldn't you have had a like instinct, if he'd had his hands in your hair? Hope couldn't read him, Donnellan didn't, Mary Kay didn't. The pair was here for going on eighteen months. Isn't such naiveté a bit like laying out guns on racks or selling ammunition by mail, and then being surprised someone kills? You don't educate kids and you're surprised they can't read? There are people out there whose lives have a trail of consequences behind them: we all repeat ourselves, Lennie and Vance did, and they left a trail. Not a soul spotted it."

She took that personally and walked out.

But then another part of Lennie's and Vance's life fell in place, thanks to the Tennessee Corrections people, who found Henning the name of a man who'd been in jail with Vance.

Henning found Frankie Esposito working as a roofer in Pennsylvania. He said he'd been coming to the end of his sentence when Vance was starting his first time in an adult prison—for molestation.

49

A lonely, scared kid, according to Frankie, and quickly turned over. Frankie said Vance got turned over regularly. Just about anyone could have dibs on him, because sex offenses were "dumb shit," everyone knew that. As if that wasn't bad enough, said Frankie, Vance thought he was cute, went about preening himself, and looked lost without a mirror, which they wouldn't allow him, because sex offenders had a high rate of suicide.

"So Warden says, can he put Vance in with me, because I'm not into that shit. Besides which, the moment he felt safe, he got himself, Vance did, a bum-buddy of his own, a pathetic sex offender called Ron, such a slob no one else wanted him. "So I said to the Warden, 'I don't want him in my hair,' and he put Vance and Ron in together."

Next thing, Frankie said, was Vance got a visit from his brother. Only Vance didn't have a brother. He didn't even have a mother or father. Then after the "brother" visited, Vance started getting letters from him.

"I used to see him in the yard. When everyone was playing ball or doing their muscle thing, Vance was mooning over this pack of letters he kept. "He looked like a broad in heat. Then one day he got hauled out to the punishment block without any time to stash his letters, and Ron passed them round to the guys for a laugh.

"We all read them," Frankie said. "Pretty high-flown shit. Like they had to be family news, you know, because letters get read before we get them or send them. So they'd be full of stuff about how lovely a younger brother had become, what this other brother was reading, quotes from books of psychology about the Greeks and love, how every young boy needed someone older and more experienced."

When Vance came out of isolation, Frankie told him to stay away from people like that, and Vance went at him for reading his letters. "The letters were sick," Frankie said.

So it hadn't been by accident that Lennie met Vance. Lennie wrote those letters; Lennie knew when Vance was coming out. And maybe had picked him inside, maybe not. But on the day he was there, waiting for him, as he said he would be.

Chapter five

On a particular Sunday marked with a big circle in Lennie's diary, Vance's "angel", Benji, was singing in the choir, and Lennie, a good-looking man not too many years off forty without ever having a thought about God, was mooching around the church only because he was curious about Vance's Jesus-fix, checking him out, figuring out if it were real. And if it were, how to deal with it.

A couple of years later, Henning, a regular churchgoer, did just what Lennie had done. Like Lennie, but happily hymning away, Henning took in the red cassocks, white surplices, and white faces of the choir. Benji's would have been as white as you could get: just a few freckles on his nose and high up on his cheeks. The red of the cassocks reddened the choir's lips. Benji's lips were full lips. He figured nothing much had changed. Pastor Samuelson was what Henning thought he'd be, a hard working man of God; the congregation was about as all-white as Samuelson was black; the choir must have been pretty much the same, only Benji had been replaced.

The service over, dazed by the brightness of the sun, Lennie had stood outside among the pick-ups and Sunday-polished cars that formed a kind of second congregation around the low brick church with its slender white steeple. His whole body hummed like a telephone wire deep in the prairie, all because he'd seen something perfect, someone who'd keep Vance happy and afford himself many a happy hour. A premonition. One of those moments that came up in his life every few years, that here was another rich experience coming his way. That was Lennie's gift, spotting the mark. Preferably someone totally private, uninvolved, willing and innocent.

He was in such a daze, he couldn't recall (but the Pastor did) shaking Samuelson's hand. What he said to Henning was that he had to fight off the various ladies whose hair-do's he recognized, who invited him coyly to lunch "some Sunday after service." He didn't want any of that, he said. "The moment I saw the boy, I knew he was ours."

Lennie found a tiny patch of shade under a recently planted tree and occupied himself with a handkerchief getting the dust off his shoes. Generally making time pass until, out back, he saw the first choir-boys and girls come out and run, in jeans and skirts and clean white shirts and blouses, towards their parents, who still stood by the front steps and the minister, talking to each other. And then out came Benji, dazzling, with no one to run to: clean and sharp, steadily walking the four blocks towards town.

For a few weeks, that became Lennie's Sunday routine: standing well back in the church (Vance always got as close to Jesus as he could) and then waiting for folks to come out, but especially the choir.

Benji, he said, was usually one of the last ones out, and it was bit by bit that Lennie learned the peculiar color of the boy's eyes, a very deep blue that bordered on violet. Likewise that Lennie became sure that the boy's folks didn't come to church, that he was alone and didn't talk to anyone, but often had a library book in his hand and went off down the street toward Maggie's Café. Everything fitted, and only someone like himself, Lennie thought, someone with his self-possession, could have waited, and thought, no, not today, maybe not even next Sunday or the one after, but soon enough.

Several Sundays, on his way back to the apartment he shared

with Vance, which was over the salon, he passed Maggie's Café, walking as slowly as possible, and saw the kid inside, reading his book in a booth, and Maggie herself serving him. Lennie liked books himself: war stories and doctor stories. He wondered what Benji's book was. Maybe he could read it himself, in preparation. He thought of going in and sitting at the counter: maybe striking up a conversation. But that wouldn't be smart. The people involved in his life had to walk in of their own accord, because he had something they wanted.

He said that at the time he blessed Homer Jacquette at the Nava County Bank. Because it was Homer who suggested that if he wanted to get ahead in Sapphire, "People here like to see local businessmen in church on a Sunday." Knowing a bit more about Vance was one good reason for going to church, but fitting in was even more important. Making everything seem natural and easy. Like becoming a part of Sapphire, showing the intention to stay, by owning property, the parcel of land and building at 304 East Houston St., for which Homer had okayed the mortgage.

Homer's face was flat, round and red. His hair was short, thin and red. He wanted badly to be thought friendly. "Should your partner sign?" Homer had asked, and Lennie, who knew Vance and his peculiarities didn't go down all that well in conservative small towns (his perpetual combing of his hair, the way he left his shirts unbuttoned down to well below his compact ribs, which in a woman would have been provocative, and in Vance, he thought with distaste, was merely vain), said if Homer meant Vance, who didn't have an ID that could fool anyone, Vance was an employee. "He just works for me," Lennie said.

At the same time he decided he wouldn't say a word about Benji to Vance. Not yet.

If at first Henning was puzzled by the nostalgia Lennie felt for his childhood, for the settled life, for "fitting" in, the better he saw into Lennie the more clearly he recognized that what Lennie missed was not the innocence of childhood, but its excitement. He wanted to experience once again the thrills of the back garden and the wood, the discovery of himself, the pleasures of his own body, and of how the world was made, which was out there just waiting to be *altered*. Childhood was a place where you could keep secrets from others. And that applied to being in church or in Jacquette's office, too. Sapphire, he thought with pleasure, was entirely unsuspecting, even unsuspicious. He had been accepted; he was even respected. The minister and the banker extended their hands to him; the ladies he cared for suggested he might want to sample some home cooking.

Henning remembered his own arrival, when he'd walked the length of Houston Street and passed by the church and school, and had his first lunch at Maggie's Café. He could as easily have fetched up there with a horse and ambled up and down Main Street at walking pace, and not have been seen. For the locals he had been someone passing through, not going to stay; going somewhere else. And had he chosen to stay, he figured it would be with him as it had been with Lennie, welcoming, maybe even enveloping.

However, this time round his walkabout took place near ten on a July night and the sky was that deep violet he associated with the Great Plains, as though the sky itself didn't quite want to sleep. Here and there TV sets flickered (Ms. Baldwin says it was after what happened that people locked their doors on hot nights). Elsewhere a yellow light might peer out from a second-floor window. But what made Sapphire the kind of community that could accommodate a Mary Kay and a Craig and a Benji, or a Lennie? Who was Mary Kay, really? Why had it all gone so badly wrong for her? The question in his mind was: If he'd been Benji, what would it have felt like to be in a place like Sapphire?

The Rapps, Henning reckoned, had simply been different. Every small town he'd ever known had its steady people and the unstable. Maybe back three, four decades when, defying her widowed father, Mary Kay had run off with her first husband, father to those children she never heard from, some disaggregation had already set in. The 'Sixties and then the war in Viet Nam would have seen to that. Yet a part of the Sapphire that was, would have gone on functioning. He had a clear memory of Mary Kay's emptied out house. It wasn't like that in the steady part of Sapphire where he was strolling. Here, where lights in upstairs windows went out one by one, no doubt husbands and wives went to it when they did, making it an occasion, but one Henning felt that would reflect respectful, comfortable love. Here couples were watched over by furniture their parents and grandparents had bought from Monkey Ward's, surrounded by flounces. Here the basements were finished and carpeted; many kept their hunting-guns down there, and spare suede jackets, comfortable old boots, and a pine-paneled bar where a man could go—if he was the occasional-drink type—and have a quick one while the wife curled up contentedly and snored. Judging from Mary Kay's submissiveness toward Craig, it wasn't like that at the Rapp place. There wasn't much comfort out where Mary Kay, Craig and Benji fought out their daily lives.

Of course, even here (in solid Sapphire) there must have been some who were alone in their houses and drank: but if so, it was because they were alone, or old, or sick. Love and loneliness were part of the pattern of their lives: the same way they dated young and knew from the start who they'd marry. But those weren't slow, steady drinkers like Mary Kay with her plum cordial and the threat of violence hanging over her.

No, there'd been another part of Sapphire, to which Mary Kay belonged. That part had gotten to know how life was elsewhere, as Mary Kay had.

Solid Sapphire, Henning thought, was the real America. But it was a diminishing America. People who lived in the big cities and on the coasts of this huge country weren't living in the same America at all. Their daughters didn't just *die* when they failed to make the Sapphire Hell-Cats Cheerleaders; Massachusetts and California daughters looked way beyond high school football and became lawyers. But at the Rapp farm—and some other places Henning had observed—there was a kind of fissure. For instance, both Mary Kay's daughters (Benji's half-sisters, whom he hardly knew or saw) had gone elsewhere as soon as they could. Because, instead of being able to buy a dress for their Proms, they'd had to send away for yards of material and more yards of tulle and run up their own dresses on an old treadle-powered sewing-machine. Nor, when they were gone from Sapphire, did they ever miss any of the sharp light-and-shadow that falls across Houston Street in Sapphire and the lives of its young. They probably wanted just what Vance thought he wanted: to be able to go to multiplexes and pick and choose flicks. In their later life, their first car was nothing much—beyond the fact it proved hard to park and they couldn't have it at college. No hours were spent underneath replacing parts or burnishing fenders the way Benji could look forward to.

When her father died and she came home without the father of those two girls, she knew she'd flunked her test as a rebel. The farm was loaded with debt and her husband had been a washout. Mary Kay, then, was stuck in a time warp. She didn't belong to the first part of Sapphire, that went on as if nothing had happened or ever would that was different from what they'd always known and liked, and she didn't belong to the second part, either. All she had was a succession of husbands or "husbands", and Homer and the other proud Sapphire people simply took more of her land every time she needed money.

When he wanted to think about Benji, Henning found himself often blocked by Lennie or Vance who, compared to a thirteen-year-old, were bigger than life. While Lennie manipulated and blended in, Vance was often bored, deeply bored. How many times had he asked Lennie, "What are you waiting for Lennie?" And always Lennie answered something like, "I don't know, something will show up." But what if nothing did?

If I were Benji, Henning thought, I'd want to get out. But wanting was one thing, doing another. Where to? How?

In that light, Benji getting together with Lennie and Vance was *providential.* Which didn't mean that the meeting, like Vance's with Lennie, wasn't *planned* as well.

When Henning went back to see Mary Kay, he had the impression another antique dealer had been by, that more stuff was gone. Like her son had gone. And neither absence was really mentioned.

The winds of change, remote as they were from Sapphire, had briefly blown through the town in the shape of Jack Broderick and his sorry group, The Banshees.

"Jack lay with me," she said, showing Henning a photograph of herself, daisies intertwined in her hair and a brick red Jack holding a guitar, "and I got myself two little girls in a row." Henning thought she was making an effort to burrow back in time and had gone right past sixteen (when Jack had lain with her) and got to six or eight. Did she really think these children had come upon her by some inattention?

In Henning's big hands, the photographed Jack trembled. One look at his black, slack hair in a ducktail, and his blank, puffy look, and Henning knew Jack had been absolutely temporary. Daddy had made Jack stay, but Jack wasn't the staying type. He went off to Florida and came back only when he needed to borrow money from Mary Kay. "I just couldn't refuse him," Mary Kay said. "I was still married to him."

"Didn't your father have anything to say about that?"

"Oh, Daddy died."

That too seemed to be by sheer carelessness. "But then you did divorce, didn't you?"

"Well... Not really. I mean... Well, you must think me very stupid, but it just didn't seem like I needed to for any particular reason. Daddy had left me a bit of money and the house and land..."

And then along came Benji's father?

Not before Jerry Zagruder ("a kind of reading man") who was good and patient with the girls but no mind at all for the farm. "Benji's father Ben came along that fall. He was a schoolteacher and we had him in to board. He must have been just fresh out of Normal, twenty-two or three, a sweet, gentle man." Then Ben got shifted to another district while Mary Kay was carrying Benji. After that, she said, things kind of went downhill for her.

Henning asked: "Benji never wondered about his father?"

"I told him he'd died." Mary Kay's hands were something like the great wisteria that climbed up her porch. Her fingers worked in and around one another, then round a handkerchief: in addition to which her hands had a slight tremble, vague as wind. "A cordial?" Mary Kay drank hers down in a gulp.

Henning felt sorry for her. Worse than the obvious *facts* of her life and Benji's, was that she had nobody to talk to. Certainly not Ms. Baldwin, nor the folks from Sheriff Overmayer's, still less the newspapermen who'd come through briefly and had done a job on her irresponsibility, and least of all Craig, on whom all her problems fell. She was less equipped than most to deal with the kind of void in which she now lived, and that too must have been hard on Benji.

"Talk to me about Benji," Henning said. "Tell me about that summer he went to work for Lennie and Vance."

She took another cordial and brought the bottle over to the dainty table between them. "I suppose you think I'm responsible for what happened, don't you? That's what everyone thinks. That I'm a rotten mother. They point at me in the street, they say she's lost three kids."

Henning said he didn't make judgments about people. But being alone the way she was, even if there was a man in the house, must have been hard on her. Surely she must have been able to see the two men were queer as three-dollar bills.

Mary Kay said she didn't know about things like that. "There was never dirty talk in this house. Not until Craig came along." If there was any change in Benji, it was that he looked lost. "I didn't think he had anyone to turn to. So I thought it was good for him to have some friends."

Well, early that summer the pair became a threesome. It seemed to Henning that both men were edgy—as if they were waiting for Benji, a Benji, someone, something, to materialize. Stretched out on the cabbage-like flowers that covered the foam-rubber mattress on the back porch's metal glider, a bottle of Dos Equis in his hand dangling over the side, for all the world a teen-ager himself, Vance asked Lennie if maybe he was planning to settle down here in Sapphire, because if Lennie was, he'd be moving on.

"And why would you even think of doing a thing like that?" said Lennie, leading him on.

"Because nothing's happening."

Sapphire wasn't giving Vance enough fun. Which was why

on his days off, and when Lennie let him, he went on to Big Fork and did dumb things. Just reading about them in the Nava County paper, Henning could see, and Lennie must also have seen, the dumb things were Vance "having fun." A hitchhiker picked up, battered and ditched; stupid mini-heists at late-night gas stations (Who else but Vance would tape up the kid on duty and take nothing more than a box of Mounds?). If sex was involved, it was always Vance's way: he never wanted, boy or girl, to see their faces. To Henning, it seemed Vance wanted to get caught. He was acting like some young wife who had got herself to the point where she was scared to stay and scared to leave.

A lot of things may have pushed Lennie's hand as the full heat of summer descended on Sapphire. Henning didn't know about them all and some of them became irrelevant, because on the Fourth of July weekend Lennie finally talked to the kid, and brought him into Hair Today. Vance's "Angel". Quite possibly the love of his life.

Here was Benji's escape. Benji didn't run, Henning thought, because he didn't love his mother, but because he did love her, and there was a part of his own nature that derived from her—a sort of acquiescence. And from his father, a part that couldn't face being responsible for Mary Kay's woes.

The truth was, Henning knew, that when one is young, one can fall in love with the color of a scarf as easily as one can with a pair of eyes, a smile, a gesture, a shyness. And Benji was ready.

First there were his Sundays, when the church bus picked him up at eight. Sundays took him into town. The music he sang worked its way into him, and the rest of the day was his, a freedom that inebriated him. Then, though every shop but one, open for the Sunday papers, cigarettes, a Coke, was shut, he could walk about town all day without Craig or his Mom telling him what to do or what was wrong with him. Those Sundays, that summer, he got to know every window and what was in it, by heart. Usually he met more than one person he knew: not his school-mates or their parents, who went home from church for their Sunday dinners, but sometimes a teacher, Father Malachy climbing into his car after mass for the Mexicans and the few other Catholics, a cop he knew or Miss Spenser who opened up the town library on Sunday afternoons and never failed to ask him how he was doing with the book he was reading. It gave him a thrill of guilt to be so free, and for people to know he was in town by himself, that the time was his to waste or spend as he wanted.

Hair Today was at the far end of his excursions up and down Houston Street, and that was where he fell in love again, this time with the picture of a girl propped in the window of the Salon. It was her hair that got to him: short, brushed back, fine, each strand catching the light. The thought that she looked like him took him several Sundays to work out, and it puzzled him. That she looked like him and not like him. He thought: I'd like to look like that.

It's natural in kids his age, people in construction, to wonder who and what they are, to see themselves in every mirror. The question was a difficult one for Benji, because in his experience of grown-ups, all that interested them was what he wanted to become (tinker, tailor, doctor, lawyer, play ball, President of the United States?), whereas he was concerned with what he was right then: reflected in the window of the Salon, a comb in his hand...

Lennie's opening line, seeing him from inside and unlocking the door suddenly, so that Benji jumped guiltily back, was: "I've seen you before. We could take care of that, you know (pointing to the comb in Benji's hand). Why don't you come on in?"

And when Benji was in the chair, Lennie called for Vance to come on down and see who was here. Vance ran his hands through Benji's hair, caressingly.

Chapter six

Throughout all the remaining Sundays that hot and dry July, Vance took the kid under his wing. At the end of the month, Lennie suggested that Benji might come and work for them Saturdays, which was always their busiest day. Then it was work from ten to ten on Saturdays, a long, deep sleep Saturday night, and "all day Sunday to play," as Lennie put it. "Though mind you, you stay with the church, the pastor counts on you." He looked at Benji as though expecting some sort of argument, the boy being attached to his mother and all that. But in fact Benji looked relieved. Apparently he'd already figured out that was where he wanted to be, which wasn't at home, so that everything Lennie had thought up seemed to be working out. He didn't even ask where he would sleep. That could be on the back porch. To start with anyway.

When service was over, Benji and Vance went all over Nava County on Vance's 50cc bike, a small one because he didn't need a license for it. Anyway, it pleased him to have Benji behind him, often with his long, slender arms around his waist. But he didn't pick him up at church, he waited (impatiently) until the boy came back and yelled up from the sparse garden—more like a parking lot—in back. This was because Lennie told him not to be obvious, and not to frighten the kid.

For the same reason, when they stopped for a swim, buck naked, in the Upper Trinity or sat around at a roadside BBQ, Vance had invented a whole new previous life for himself, in which there was nothing that could frighten or shock the boy, mostly just the early part, what it was like growing up with your folks dead and shunted from place to place. He also talked extensively about Jesus, and how he felt Jesus knew everything he did, how He was a comfort, and also you had to watch out for Him, because He knew everything you did.

As a matter of fact, these were things Vance was beginning to think out for himself, and having the boy around to talk to was a help. When he came to things in his past he shouldn't have done (ever!), Vance caught himself hesitating, as though those things would hurt Benji too, and therefore shouldn't have happened.

He gave the boy plenty of space, so he didn't feel pressed, only occasionally, as though it were the most natural thing in the world, walking with him hand-in-hand. This sort of airiness and space was curiously relieving; even more relieving, he soon noticed, was not having Lennie about, watching.

Of course Lennie always wanted to know, Sunday night after he drove the boy back home to Mary Kay's (never stopping, though always invited if Craig wasn't there), what had gone on. To the last detail, Lennie found it frankly funny that on these occasions Vance neither bragged nor pretended. Just their being together, he and Benji, was quite good enough, at least for now. Lennie thought he was being like a bashful boy who wouldn't admit he was falling in love. But he didn't kid Vance about it. Henning thought, maybe it reminded Lennie of times when he had been Vance's age, or even Benji's.

None of that ease, however, kept Vance from imagining things that might happen. If he ever thought of the boy naked as he jumped gleefully into the river, or the times he had stood in the backyard waiting by moonlight for the single sheet to fall off the boy as he slept on the back porch on the relentlessly hot nights, seeing the white skin where his pants had always covered him up, the tight, high buttocks, the still sparsely blond-haired pubis, then Jesus reminded him sharply and he rolled over on his belly to drive the boy away.

He said to Jesus that he couldn't help himself. He didn't ask for these images to crowd into his mind, or for his body to react.

What he did instead, to calm himself down, was listen to Lennie groan from the single bed up the hall, tossing and turning restlessly, some operetta playing, lately *Fledermaus*.

Lennie tracked Vance's thought. He knew what Vance was thinking. He needed to know, and his notebooks showed, cryptically, week by week, how Vance was falling for the boy.

Henning asked himself if Lennie would have been writing so candidly if he were acting with malice aforethought.

Henning felt he was coming to grips with Vance's problem—at least in those early, idyllic days. The boy was remote from Vance. You could touch him, frolic with him, feel him, but Benji wasn't really there. He lived in some vague terrain far away from the very real world in which Vance lived, and Lennie operated. That was because, like many adolescents, Benji was enamored of himself and his new "look". It was himself he loved, not Vance.

Lennie saw it too. He caught the boy looking at himself in the bright-bulbed salon mirrors, in Vance's eyes, and even in the eyes of the Saturday customers, who often gave him generous tips for their shampoos. The look in Benji's eyes was one of gratification, and the salon was a dream world in which little events took place without him knowing how or why. It was a place of transformations: customers patiently submitted themselves to the collective care of Hair Today in order to make themselves attractive to others. And he was learning, Lennie wrote.

Lennie also caught the language, of looks, of winks and smiles, between Benji and Vance.

Well obviously, thought Henning, putting his heap of Xeroxed copies of Lennie's notebooks aside. Of course Benji knew that Vance "desired" him, though he might have had no real idea what that meant. Still, there was no doubt he would have sensed the heat Vance gave off, his constant physical presence, the way he leaned over his shoulder to whisper some instruction, the little lessons he gave on how to walk less awkwardly, or the clothes he bought him that were softer and better suited to his long legs and elegant arms. All these things added up. They may have seemed entirely casual, but the boy felt that bit by bit he, too, was being pleasantly transformed, that he too could be an object of love and be attractive to another. He trusted Vance completely: not to do anything too open or obvious of which he might be afraid. Henning thought: they were in Lennie's secret garden, and like any pair of adolescents, secretly, pleasurably, frightened of one another.

Lennie told Vance, and noted: "Take your time. When the apple is ripe, it falls from the tree."

Throughout that first summer of Benji's that Henning read about, that haunted him, Henning himself revisited his own premonitions, the things he had feared for his own son, Luca, long after Ludi had left him and taken Luca with her. Sometimes, the two boys became one, Luca like a dark angel and Benji a bright, more conventional one. Premonitions never promised anything good. They weren't déjà *vu*, they were *pas encore vu*, things that would happen, and the more terrifying for that, because you couldn't stop them happening.

Did Vance plan the next move? Or was it Lennie who staged it, by saying one Friday in early August, when Benji had been long out of school and spent all the time he could at the Salon, that his mother had called to say she was ill, and that he was flying out West to be with her? Henning was doubtful. More likely it was Lennie's pills that did it, which were always plentiful. Didn't one's moods need constant altering? Was anything, ever, *absolutely* right?

The three of them drove to Amarillo and dropped Lennie off at the airport, but did Lennie really go? Henning, who spent hours going through computer records for the day, never found any Crace traveling, anywhere. Though that didn't mean Lennie hadn't used another name. He spent three days there checking the ticket counters with a photograph of Lennie, with no result. Lennie looked so perfectly Middle American it would have been a wonder if any of the girls working the desks remembered him. In Amarillo, Henning was able to establish that Vance and Benji had registered as brothers and shared a room in the YMCA downtown. Henning went and sat in the very Coffee Shop where things had started.

The decor was lugubrious. The seats had rips in their Leatherette; the chrome-and-Formica tables were unbalanced. There was a strong smell of chlorine from the swimming pool in the basement. There, Henning had better luck. Several people remembered the "brothers", one because he'd heard about the case and seen Vance's picture in the papers. "There was a third one with them, a huge biker."

Ronald Homolka, "Captain Ron", forty-one arrests—drunk and disorderly, Driving Under the Influence, flashing, child molestation, soliciting—unhealthy, fat, always unshaven. Tennessee Corrections e-mailed Henning the picture. It was Ron all right. Vance's bum-buddy, the man who more or less sold Vance to Lennie and who, on this little foray, did indeed sport the bandy legs and gear of a real biker: the high boots, the studded leather jacket and leggings, the earrings, the beer belly and the don't-give-a-shit look.

The question was, who sent for Captain Ron? It could have been Vance, who might have heard from Ron, or kept in touch with him since they had done time together. If one thinks of Vance getting excited (the pills, but also the long frequentation of Benji), or even impatient, wanting to get to the "next stage", then Vance was the most likely. Lennie could have put the idea in his head. For all Henning knew, as everyone was someone else at that party, Lennie could have been there, and it wasn't at all certain anyone would have recognized him.

Henning thought Lennie. It was much more Lennie's scene.

Lennie would have known where Vance would go in Amarillo. He went to the Y any chance he got. So he could have told Ron where they'd be, and of course Vance would act as though seeing Ron was a great surprise.

Most of the tables in the cafeteria were empty. Ron rolled right up and sat down opposite Vance. He said, "Move over, Kid," and shoved Benji up against the wall.

Benji looked across the table at Vance to work out how he should behave.

Vance gave Ron his shit-eating grin: "Ron!" They'd have given each other the usual high-five or something like that, and then Ron would have studied Benji: bleary-eyed, could be, but also prudent. Both Ron and Vance were familiar with the game. Ron wouldn't have picked out any single feature in the boy—not the delicate mouth, the snub nose, the few freckles—but he would have played the game the way it was always played, laughed and got up to get something to eat, taken his wine from the brown paper bag under his seat, swigged at it, and self-confident now, leered and said: "You ever been kissed, boy?"

"Yessir."

"By your Ma."

"Yessir."

"Yessir, Captain Ron."

"Yessir, Captain Ron."

"You enjoy your dinner, boy?"

"Yessir… Captain Ron."

Vance said, then, not really looking at Benji, but round the room, as though there were lots of people listening, instead of just the Black woman who handed out the food that came from a little hatch behind her, and then ladled out the stuff that was in long metal trays: "Ron was in 'Nam," he said.

"What'ya say to that, boy?" asked Ron, putting his arm round Benji's shoulder.

Said Vance: "He's a fucking hero, Benji. A loyal, patriotic American who did his duty. What do girls do when heroes come home from the wars?"

"Kiss 'em," said Ron. "Seems like you're my date for tonight, boy. We're going to have ourselves a ball! And I ain't your Ma, right?"

"Right."

"Right, Captain Ron."

"Right Captain Ron."

He had a huge, booming voice. His head was just as big, with long, dirty hair that he nestled in Benji's neck. Vance was laughing. "Give him a kiss then!"

Captain Ron would have puckered his lips and held them out for the boy, and Benji would have shut his eyes and done what he'd been told to do.

"Shall we…?" said Vance, getting up.

The boy must have known then that Vance wasn't going to protect him. Vance was looking the other way. He wanted to get going and he wouldn't even look at Benji.

But was Benji aware, Henning asked himself, that he'd stepped across a frontier, and was now in some country where he didn't know the rules?

Then came the awful next questions, which were: what would his son Luca have done, and what did he do? And what would he himself have done? At thirteen? The first one Henning found too painful to look at too closely, aware as he was that when he'd first read in a magazine about Lennie and Vance and Benji, the story—innocence corrupted—had leapt from the page and, much as he'd suppressed it, had forced him to go to Sapphire and *at least* take a look.

As for himself at thirteen, it was all very well to say he wasn't a Benji or anything like him—that he hadn't fallen in love with his own looks, that he hadn't felt particularly out of place in Alva, Oklahoma (though you read a whole lot of books), that he hadn't had an overly doting mother (didn't have one at all that very year of thirteen, nor a father), that he hadn't doubted that he'd soon enough work his way into Betty Sue Fregosa's panties and then past them, and that if there were any queers in that town they were well and wisely hidden. The question remained, what does a kid do, especially when his best friend has just betrayed him, faced with the peremptory nature of a grown-up who knows no rules and can do whatever he wants with you?

Henning's answer was, he clams up. Henning thought, I would

have shut up and hoped nothing bad would happen, or my friend had a plan, or someone would see us. I'd think, no, he can't touch me; he's not my father, not my mother, not my friend.

But wait a minute. This kid's already been necking with Vance. He already knows, more or less, that guys can kiss each other.

In the back seat of the taxi that was taking them wherever they were going, Captain Ron had his right hand held tight to the zip on his leather pants, his other hand grasped Benji's head and tried to force it down into his lap, which was spread wide. But that was impossible just then, there wasn't room enough. The boy didn't say a thing. He was squeezed between Vance and his friend, and Vance's friend was a Hero. He looked at Vance. Vance's face, caught in the headlights of oncoming traffic, was a shiny, white moon. Silent as a moon.

Was Benji excited? Henning asked himself. More excited, less afraid? Or not at all excited and more scared?

The taxi left them off in front of a high, modern building with a big lobby and a marble floor. There they were stopped at the door by an officious Black doorman (with a badge that read "Concierge" on the breast pocket of his blazer) until permission for their entry was ascertained by telephone.

"This way, Mr. Homolka," said the doorman, leading them to one of three elevators. It said "Penthouse Only."

Once inside they rose swiftly in subdued light and a curious fragrance until the doors opened and Vance stepped out, then Ron, blinking at the brightness, then Benji hidden behind them.

Henning concentrated on seeing things through Benji's eyes. Who saw Captain Ron go one way into a kind of drawing room big as a swimming pool, and Vance being immediately led away by their hostess (if she were a woman, which Vance later said—for whom the whole party was a gas—wasn't sure, she was a short, stout woman in a dark dress and tightly crimped hair), not to reappear for several minutes while Benji stood there, not knowing what to do.

Next there was a burst of applause as Vance re-entered as Bette Davis, with very heavy eyelids, a cigarette in her hand, and a husky voice. She took Benji by the hand and led him into the drawing room, which Benji saw had a huge outdoor terrace, too, and a view in every direction of the city sprawled out thirty floors below them, like a scattering of yellowing stars. Vance wore a tight-bodiced, wide-skirted dress of some shiny, dark red material with elongated red fingernails to match. He brought two glasses with him and gave one to Benji, dropping his voice in order to whisper in his ear all the compliments he'd already had about him—things like, from their hostess, "What a darling little boy!" Somewhere, a band was playing. Smoke rose from a barbecue tended by two waitresses in black satin with white pinafores; both had powerful, muscular arms.

The room and the terrace were full of couples dancing, most of the "girls" in short dresses and elaborate hair-do's, the "boys", some of them, in white Mexican shirts and trousers that shone like silk. Captain Ron was by them, using his big hands to slam a steak down on a piece of bread.

"Who are all these people?" Benji whispered back to Vance. "Do I have to be Captain Ron's 'date'? You're my friend."

"It's Captain Ron's party," Vance said. "You're his date. You should be flattered."

"I need to go to the bathroom."

Vance led him there and had him wash his face and brush his teeth. Then hugged him consolingly, the way his mother would have. "The first time on a date is always tough," he said. "Then you'll get to want it."

Still later, Captain Ron also led him to the bathroom, but this one marked "Powder Room." There was a very tall and skinny girl in there, and huge cupboards with dresses on hangers. "Everyone here is someone else," said Ron. "That's the idea. Rachel here will hang your clothes up. Come on, get undressed. And drink up."

When he had finished his glass, Ron refilled it. Rachel meanwhile had found a little short dress of red silk and put Benji's thin arms through its sleeves. Then she brought him over to the washbasins and, taking a brush, carefully applied lipstick to his lips.

Ron led him out on the floor to dance, which Benji had never done. But Ron moved him round and round until Benji was giddy.

One of the big waitresses came over with two glasses on a tray and Ron gave him one to drink, sitting him down on a huge leather sofa while couples stopped by to say how pretty he was.

The drink sparkled in Benji's glass and he realized it was champagne. He said, which was the first time he spoke to Ron: "My mother dreams about champagne, she wants to go to Italy." It made sense to say something to this huge man. But talking made him even giddier, and he looked around the room, trying to find Vance.

When Captain Ron left for a moment, Benji got up and walked around the room twice amongst the couples, but couldn't find Vance, though he saw someone who looked vaguely like him, far away, by the piano. Now Vance's cigarette was in a long holder and the hand holding it was in a long white glove. He was singing in a husky voice. Next to him Captain Ron was bent over a low table with a straw in his nose.

Much later, in his own clothes, he woke up in a bed with Vance, no longer Bette Davis, asleep beside him.

Sunday night they, but not yet Lennie, were back in Sapphire. Benji nestled comfortably beside Vance on the glider, sharing a bottle of Dos XX. Vance explained how it had been with him the first time. It was better to accept being the girl, he said, and even be grateful.

Benji said he was grateful it was Vance he woke up with, not Ron. Vance said: "Look, you know it couldn't be me."

Henning thought: No, Benji didn't know that, but after Ron, he knew where his real home was. Wherever Vance was. It was there in black-and-white in the brief diary Benji kept: "He was wearing perfume which made him smell the same as Mom."

Chapter seven

One of the most difficult things for Henning Forsell was the light in Sapphire, its picture-postcard daylight, pure blue and blinding white. In his life, light meant good things. Same for most people.

He sat talking about that with Mrs. Spenser on a Sunday afternoon in the makeshift town library. The sun burned right through the blinds and hurt his eyes. But she'd been a friend to Benji. A good friend.

It wasn't that he liked talking about such things, but he felt that somehow the town had turned its back on Benji. It didn't want to hear about him or think about him. And for some reason that had to do with the light. It rubbed things out.

He said that Jack the Ripper ripped in the dark and rapists performed in neglected parts of parks, even serial killers cut up body parts in cellars. "We think dark crimes and dark places go together. We find it hard to acknowledge crime in our own daylight. You know, where there are errands to be done; mustn't forget the shopping, the car needs oil."

A sensible, low-shod woman, widowed young, she had rich, curly black hair and a pleasant, throaty laugh. "Light and dark and Benji Rapp," she said. "That's interesting. I suspect some people are vulnerable whatever the weather."

"Victims maybe," Henning answered. "But not the people who commit crimes. Fully awake, sentient, clear-headed, neither drunk nor drugged, the sun up, the air clean and bright, who kills another, unless there's rage?"

It appalled him. Vance and Lennie lived in the fullest light. Not just was Hair Today fluorescent, so was the Sapphire sky: white, hot and flat. Lennie, particularly, was lucid. As far back as he could remember he had been lucid. Everything in his head was luminous, clear, and that was the way he liked it. Floodlit.

Yet for all that light, no one had seen what was coming.

"You had no sense of it at all? In class? When Benji came in here for his stock of books?"

"I didn't. No. I thought, if anything, Benji seemed happy enough. Maybe happy to be away from home. As most young people are, to have some sort of line drawn around them, so they know where they are. He never got that at home with Mary Kay and Craig."

But Henning had walked Houston Street every day for a couple of months now. He knew, from looking in himself—even though the salon had shut down and was for rent—that you could, from the street, as Benji once had, look into the Salon and see everything that was going on.

On a typical weekend all three of them would have been at work: Lennie darting about his customers, light on his feet, studying their hair from all angles, holding up mirrors to show how brilliantly he'd arranged curls to show their slender necks, dancing about them as he accompanied them to the cash register, zapping their credit cards through the machine, listening to the near inaudible crunch of its micro-printer, proffering a ball-point, gold in color, for them to sign; or Vance, more studied, closer to the ground, perhaps with more flair, fluffing coiffures he'd learned from the fashion magazines he devoured with a steady flow of chatter, the sorts of "That's lovely, darling" remarks they expected of queers, paying close attention to the considered opinions of his mostly younger customers who knew exactly the "look" they wanted, what supermodels they had the gifts to be, or what wholesome girls in search of partners for life with good jobs.

Towards the back in those days you would have seen Benji, slight and dancing like Lennie, but shorter, an assiduous listener like Vance, blond too, sweeping up the hair that gathered in hassocks like lumps of prairie grass, supplying the towels that lay across the customers' shoulders or taking them out to the laundry bin. It was Benji who prepared the dyes and the gold- or silver-foil papers that held hair in place within the curlers, who kept order, served coffee, took away and emptied ashtrays, and wrapped towels in turbans around the freshly-shampooed heads of the ladies of Sapphire, most of whom knew him and asked after Mary Kay and school and his singing. It was Benji too who stood with Lennie when a hair-do was done, dried, brushed out, arranged by Lennie or Vance, and gave an honest, frank (but favorable) opinion on how the ladies looked.

Behind him, past the basins for shampooing, the rack for coats in winter, was the kitchen you could see right through to the tall and narrow windows that gave onto the yard at back, itself divided into strips of parked cars: Lennie's Subaru and the variety of the CUSTOMERS ONLY parking. No dark there, either.

Nor was Vance a creature of the night. He dressed for daylight, brightly, in soft Hawaiian shirts unbuttoned down to the navel. He sauntered down the main drag wanting to be seen. Mirrors, plate glass, even chrome, seduced him. By the bright bulbs in the salon he preened himself. His Mod Op for petty crime was daylight robbery. He did his stuff by day. More fun to wire a car in a mall parking lot—carrying a laden shopping bag and looking like an ordinary Joe straight out of Sears—with everyone looking on, scratching his head and saying, "Must be the sparks..." People were dumb and unthinking, the world full of suckers.

"Daylight," Henning said in conclusion, "is where habits flourish." It was where Vance, twenty-three, and Benji, thirteen, accomplished their connections to one another. Night was the natural time for predators. They have senses that are in full operation at all times, they have an eye for pouncing. Set off a firecracker next to a ruminant and it hardly turns its head—too busy browsing.

"It's at night that Lennie brought out his pills," Henning said. "He likes risk. You study him, you'll see each time the risk is greater and the more he likes it."

It seemed to Henning that with Vance restless, the hunt had become an end in itself. What Lennie had done with Vance was domesticate his prey. "Lennie led Vance onto the floor, Vance was a willing partner."

Lately Henning had come across Miss Tabitha Perkins, a lady well into her sixties whose tongue wagged—as a cow's ears flap non-stop during the high season of flies. She lived in a little one-story house two blocks south of Houston Street, at the limits of the town's expansion around the time of the Great War when the railroad came through Nava County. She was a spinster of the sort there are always some of in small towns like Sapphire: women who for one reason or another—either it's their choice or, too young to know better, had once set their minds on someone entirely unsuitable—and then remained shelved for the rest of their natural lives.

She was a regular at Hair Today and at Maggie's Café, which was where Henning got to talking to her—in fact, she came over and sat down at his booth, saying, "You must be Mr. Forsell. I hear about you all the time. Maybe you'll listen to me more than all those lawyers and that lazy Sheriff, because I'll tell you one thing, maybe all the rest of the folks round here were shocked and surprised by what those men did, but I wasn't. You'd have to be real dumb not to see what was going on with that young Benji boy in that salon of theirs. They quarreled all the time, Lennie and Vance, and it was always about Mary Kay's boy, the son of that weak and silly man Mary Kay took up with, that school-teacher."

"What did they quarrel about?" Henning asked.

"They were like two boys quarreling over a girl, but there was something weird about it, Vance being what you people back East call 'gay', and Lennie not being that way at all, 'least in my opinion. There was some other game he was playing, and you just knew it involved Vance and the boy. Lennie would tease Vance, Vance would tease the boy. Then Lennie would turn on Vance and Vance would say he wanted out—Out of what? is what I ask. There had to be something going on. Mary Kay trusted Lennie, she told me that plenty of times. It's Vance who was the little pervert. Dan Overmayer wouldn't listen to me. I said to him, 'Sometime, somewhere, that young man did something really terrible, and it's going to happen again.' Of course he paid me no heed."

"How did you know that?"

"I just knew it. I used to watch his hands in the mirror when he was doing my hair. They're the hands of someone who's done something. They never relaxed, those hands, like they were trying to wash something out. He giggled and jiggled; his hands did too. So I took my hair fixing to Lennie. And I told him why. He just smiled and said not to worry, that he could handle Vance. I told Mary Kay, too. But she's got that man on her hands, his drinking and all, and how could you do anything with a boy Benji's age these days? And she was right in a way. They were all in that game *together*. That's what I wanted to say. What's that word lawyers use, 'accomplices'? No, accessories. Benji's Ma and Craig too."

She talked too much, she was too sure of herself, but Henning thought in many ways she was right. There were probably awful things in Vance's past. To have screwed him up so badly. Probably in Lennie's too. And Lennie was on his mind. Everything in Henning's experience had taught him that no person is so opaque, so indecipherable, as one who is in love with himself.

Vance might have been a narcissist, but Lennie loved everything about himself. He sat on the edge of his cot and inhaled deeply of his socks as he took them off. He felt fragrant, down to armpits and underpants. In the mirror he examined his teeth, picked and flossed. They were perfectly regular, small and even utterly admirable. As were his ears, which were delicate and shapely. He tended to himself as a careful servant polishes the silver in his custody: his person—impeccable; his speech—cultivated, but sometimes adopting the common touch; his manner—languid, laid back; his look—casual.

He thought of himself as beautifully self-made, and how could he be interested in the common clay of others?

Perhaps, despite the temptation to speak about himself, it took Lennie several months to agree to see Henning; and when he did, he had rules as to what he would talk about and what he wouldn't. He wanted Henning to know he was far too intelligent to talk pop psychology the way the state's shrinks had done: he wasn't crazy, he knew exactly what he was doing; and if it hadn't been for Vance, he'd probably be "out there somewhere much more comfortable for a conversation."

"Could be," said Henning, who wasn't easily impressed. "I've been thirty years doing what I do, and if there's one thing I've learned, it's that people like you, who think they're totally in charge, live in a world of their own making. I suspect you know no other truth than your own truth, and I know damn well you'll only give up any of it bit by bit, when it suits your purpose."

Lennie, sitting across the table in one of the lawyers' rooms, smiled confidently. "The fact is, we're sitting in here," Lennie said. "I'm going to be here a fair while, so why should I talk to you?"

Henning lit a cigarette and passed one to Lennie. "Beats boredom, I'd say. You tell me why you said yes to my request."

"I heard you'd been around. Definitely not minding your own business. You seem to be able to do pretty much as you please. Also, my lawyer said you'd been around home. I don't like that. My folks don't deserve to get hurt."

"Just a telephone call. So far."

"What did they tell you?"

"Your father only. Said he didn't want to talk about you."

In fact, that one call had been a testy affair. Only Crace's father had turned up at the trial. He had given one or two interviews and then gone back west. On the phone, Henning had said all he wanted to talk about was long ago, when Lennie was a kid—before he had married Hope. Mr. Crace was polite but distant. Henning said he was going to see Lennie: did he want to send him any message? Since Lennie didn't seem to be getting any mail from home, was Lennie's mother at least getting the letters Lennie had been writing?

There had been no answer to that, so Henning said he'd give Lennie their regards, and that was that. Which he did. And Lennie said, very cool, "What did you want to ask my Dad?"

"Your childhood…"

"Have you been reading my notebooks?"

Henning saw no reason to lie. "Someone called Hal," he replied. "He's in there. Along with your garden and the boy who'd been punished for spilling ink. Who was Hal?"

That visit, Lennie didn't want to talk about Hal. Nor the next visit. Then, instead, he sent Henning a long, handwritten letter, which more or less had the following to say.

Hal Borglund was his name. He was an outdoorsman. He hunted, he scouted, and he had Indian stories to tell. He wore high socks and khaki shorts and a shirt full of pockets, and his bag, Lennie wrote, was kids. You had a Little League to organize—he was it. Same with football and basketball, same with the YFA, the Young Farmers.

Three, four times a year he took a half-dozen kids on real treks along the Republican River, sometimes as far as over the state line round the dam at Bonny Reservoir. He was a tough nut on physical stuff, walking behind the boys, telling them to 'swing them hips' or 'stretch those legs'. He seemed to like the discomfort, the smell of mildewed rubber ground sheets, getting kids to compete—who could find the most dry wood, start a fire quickest without a match. The best at all those tests became Head Boy. That was something you competed for: Head Boy got extras, Head Boy got to share tent or cabin with Hal.

"You know the game called "hunting the snipe"? The snipe is a mythical bird. There's no such bird as a snipe, but you don't know that. Around the campfire, the youngest, the most innocent, is set the task of finding the snipe. It is a matter of being absolutely still and watching carefully, and when the snipe is found, calling out to your companions. Of course, by then, the older kids who've set out on the hunt with you are all back in their tents laughing their heads off at how dumb you are."

Well it seemed that Lennie had been about Benji's age, his first time out, somewhere miles out on a slope. The forest rose above him. The campsite, with its comforting lights and its smell of roasting hot dogs, was invisible but, he thought, over that way. He lay hunkered down in his covert, senses alert, the mythical snipe's mating call—often repeated round the campfire—firmly impressed on his ear. Waiting. And then waiting some more. Then, over the hill, the first of many hills, the sun sank and with it went the lingering warmth in bark and forest floor. In no time it was dark; in less than no time at all, a late-fall chill set in. The forest fell silent, though occasionally a branch snapped, a bough stirred, some creature slithered among the pine needles and twigs.

The obligation had been absolute. He had promised to be faithful. He would find a snipe.

The moon had risen. He had continued to strain his ears for the sound the snipe was supposed to make, a sort of sorry-sounding whistle that starts high and goes down and down. It got cold and he was hungry. But he hadn't dared give up, though by now, having not heard a human voice in hours, he'd started walking around and worrying that he might be lost.

When, at last, exhausted from clambering around and desperately hungry, he had stumbled back to the camp, the only light on was in Hal's cabin. Into which he crept quietly in search of food, a piece of bread, anything.

The cabin had two rooms: the front room where they would gather in bad weather and where supplies were kept, and a room in back, with two beds. A pale yellow light seeped out of the back room, as well as the sound of sobbing, to which, at first, he paid little attention. As he moved furtively about among the stacked boxes of tins, fumbling with his fingers for the waxy wrappings of the bread loaves, a draft of wind shifted the door between the two rooms open, more light seeped out, the sobs became louder, and Lennie turned around, afraid of being seen.

Hal stood between the two beds, his legs clamped together, muscles bulging, his shorts in a khaki pool at his feet. Kneeling in front of him was the Head Boy, his head bobbing.

"Hal's eyes," Lennie wrote, "were wide open, staring straight at me helplessly, like he was imploring me, begging me, and I knew I was supposed to go away, not to have seen anything. He didn't move at all. His mouth was hanging half open, he seemed to be having trouble breathing, and the sobbing I heard was him taking a breath. You understand?"

Henning understood. Lennie had the man in his power. Hal couldn't move or do anything. He was on the edge.

"It was his eyes though that got me and, when I looked down, the close-cut back of the Head Boy's head. Hal was looking right at me. We were having a conversation with our eyes. On my side, threat and excitement; on his, fear and doubt. All sorts of things were being laid out for me to take. Head Boy? Did I want to do what this one was doing, jammed up against Hal's crotch? Was it money I wanted? Would I burst into tears and run away?"

None of the above, obviously, Henning decided. He said not an effing word. Not then, not the next day, not ever. That way he *owned* Hal. That is, if Lennie were? telling the truth. But Henning thought it was probably the way Lennie would have *liked* it to happen.

Chapter eight

The subject of Mary Kay Rapp and Craig came up enough times during Sunday lunch at Pastor Samuelson's house to let Henning know two things: that the Preacher, deeply black, stern and six feet six tall, didn't mince his words, and that he thought he'd somehow failed Benji. After twenty years as a dean in a small Black college, Samuelson had come late to the ministry; he had a young (white) wife; he carved a blade of beef like a surgeon; and made it plain to Henning he found it damned difficult to be charitable towards all. He said: "I wouldn't want you to think we were all deaf and blind here, Mr. Forsell. The Lord didn't make me the sort of man who can easily forgive folly. And fools is what Mary Kay and Craig and lots of others round here are."

He was down on Craig for going 'round town threatening "those goddam faggots," Lennie and Vance. Shoot, who didn't know Craig was an unhappy drunk who hated himself for taking the easy way and fixing himself up with Mary Kay? He was down on Mary Kay for dumping yet another "Dad" on the boy.

"Could have been otherwise if she'd had any sense," he said.

"Truth is, Craig's crazy about kids, but because of Viet Nam he can't have any."

His wife, with her long, straight blond hair and fine, clear skin, added that she often thought Craig had taken up with Mary Kay on account of the kid.

"That's right," continued Samuelson. "You could see how hurt he was when the boy refused to recognize *any* of the things Craig did for him. Like keeping his Ma on her own property, like trying to be a good Dad for Benji, or just for caring.

"When he drinks he can't handle things."

His wife said apologetically, Sapphire had more than its fair share of "Nam wreckage." "Like those junked cars you see out by the Mexicans. They had a purpose once, now they're rotting from the inside."

Mary Kay wasn't much better. Sometimes Samuelson thought she might be just plain feeble-minded. She rarely had two thoughts in a row that added up.

He said that just about every Sunday he saw Benji hurry away through the parking lot to his beloved hairdressers, couldn't get there fast enough, never wanted to go home. "But if I were to talk harsh to Mary Kay Rapp, I knew she'd just fold up shop. She's not a real parishioner; she comes maybe once a month when Crag will let her have his pick-up. Most I could ever do was ask her how the boy was, how much she saw him those days, what he did when he was at home, that sort of stuff. I just hoped one day she'd say something or ask for advice. If she did that, well it was just possible I could bring her into the real world.

"Fat chance. Not just that she didn't ask for help, she just *couldn't* answer even a simple question about the boy. Anything you said to her, hurt her. I mean physically. Benji was her flesh and blood. You said something about Benji, you were saying something about her. I tell you, Mr. Forsell, that poor woman's got a heavy investment in defeat. Never had much luck with her kids or her husbands, what's she got left? Benji. She'd look distracted and mumble something about Benji being fine; he'd be fine, he was a good boy. Last time I saw her, the day before that crazy man, the biker, came to town, I hear, with that red dress, I asked her here, to share our lunch. Oh no, she couldn't, Craig had to have his food on the table and this and that. She got so flustered I knew she didn't have any idea what Benji was up to. Whatever she'd seen at all she made sure she'd forget."

It was a pattern, Samuelson said. She never saw a disaster coming. "It's the hardest virtue, hope." Samuelson said. "Yet there was a woman who had hope as I'd like to have it. She truly thought her husbands would turn out good men, that Craig tried hard, that the boy would turn out all right. What do you do with forlorn hope like that, Mr. Forsell? You take it away from them? The one thing they've got?

"Well. In the end," the pastor said bitterly, just when Henning thought he'd finished, "I didn't have to take it away from her, did I? She lost it all by herself."

As Samuelson recounted, by the end of that summer, when school started up again, things had gone way beyond whether Benji should drink his milk or do his chores. Sunday night to Friday morning, the question was how to get through to the boy at all. He came home, did his school work, sat down at table with Mary Kay chatting away about art and all, put away his dinner in five minutes, saying nothing because Craig was there, and then went upstairs and shut himself up in his room.

She said, going up the stairs, knocking on his door, "Benji honey, we're your family, you're being very hurtful."

Family maybe. But not the family he wanted. He stayed silent. If she insisted, wanting badly to give him a hug, he'd come to the door and ask how the hell he fitted in with this house, with the man she'd taken up with, having nothing to do, always being told to do this and not do that, Craig saying he was some sort of misfit. "Maybe I don't fit," he said. "One day I might just not come back."

"You ought to tell Mr. Forsell about when he fainted," Mrs. Samuelson said, cutting up pecan pie.

"Mr. Means, he's the choir master—came to me one Sunday and told me the boy had fainted during practice, passed out. I called

Mary Kay. I told her it wasn't just puberty or the heat. Mr. Means said the boy took a lot of rousing, and when he did come to, he wouldn't let Means call Doctor Szendeffy. I hate to say this, Mr. Forsell, but Sarah and I thought he'd been taking something."

"What did she say?"

Samuelson shrugged. "What do you think she said? She said Benji wasn't that kind of boy, he'd never been in trouble."

"That was it?"

"No. I questioned Means some more, and he said that lately, after one Sunday he missed altogether without telling anyone, Benji had been coming late."

The Sunday he missed, Henning guessed, was the weekend Lennie supposedly went out West.

Sarah Samuelson was more gentle. Her husband had had many children by his first wife, she said. It was remembering them that hurt him about Benji, the feeling he'd had that summer that something had changed in Benji. "He was a beautiful, bright-eyed boy," she said. "And so open. I'd watch him myself, and I loved it when he had a solo. Then suddenly he wouldn't talk to anyone. He was contemptuous of people like us, of adults generally. I don't know if it was that he didn't want advice, that he didn't trust us, or if it was simpler than that, that he didn't want anyone prying into his life."

"There were signs enough," Samuelson said. "Sometimes I thought he was in real pain. He walked differently, his eyes had become expressionless, and sometimes his lips trembled. The sort of thing you couldn't entirely say were just symptoms of puberty, of growing up, the natural shyness that comes over boys at his age. And there was Mary Kay talking all those problems away into dreamland. May the Lord forgive all of us."

Walking back to the Tam O'Shanter from his copious lunch, Henning wondered what the hell anyone could have done. The incline was steep. Benji tumbled. Benji was pushed.

No one followed up on the pills. But then, at the time, no one knew about the porn, either. That didn't come up until the trial. They were found in a neat parcel in Benji's closet, inside a blue canvas bag that had once held Craig's bowling ball. Hard stuff, glossy enlargements of engrossed organs and gaping apertures shaded with hair, that Ms. Baldwin held up to the jurors at arms' length. Were they even Benji's?

Pam hadn't hesitated to use them to show how the boy had been "depraved" by the defendants, and Judge Perkins, Miss Perkins' younger brother, Henning recalled, had chided her for bringing such things into a courtroom. But had anyone asked what Benji could possibly have made of them?

The pills, on the other hand, were both plentiful and evident. Even if the boy hadn't passed out in choir practice. Most people Henning talked to knew about them. Certainly in connection with Vance. Hell, afterwards Craig said Vance passed them round Friday nights at the VFW and bragged about how his buddy, Lennie, could get anything he wanted. They were what everyone used: uppers and downers, analgesics, muscle-relaxants, anti-inflammatories, steroids, hormones, each a precious part of the rich, self-remedying pharma-copoeia of modern America.

And clearly, plus much harder stuff, they were part of the rich decor of Ron's "party" in Amarillo, which of all the trio's "adventures", Henning considered far and away the most significant. How to look at it? The Kid had passed out, come to in Vance's bed, and had no idea what happened to him in between? He knew but didn't want to talk about it?

The scenario Henning came up with was based on the fact that Benji never said no to the boys.

Lennie or Vance said, clean up, he cleaned up; go here, go there, fetch this, hop in. It was all the same to Benji. He'd signed up.

They were going to see Lennie off in Amarillo? Fine. Benji got in the Subaru with his new buddies, he was stuck in the back seat, but he saw places he'd never seen.

Lennie was a notoriously slow driver. Seat belt buckled, prim, making Vance do the same. He used the two-lane blacktop all the way, and kept flipping the dial, county to county, place to place. The landscape drained away through the windows; Benji watched, half asleep in the heat of an unairconditioned car, the windows open, the heat flowing heavily onto his eyelids. He saw grassland, signs that led to Pueblo ruins, to the Boy's Ranch. It must have been like having run off with the circus, with gypsies, or plain just having run away.

They reached Amarillo along State 1061 and crawled through town to the airport on the far side, Vance mum until Lennie slid out with his bag and tossed Vance the keys. No hugs from Lennie. He didn't touch people.

Vance drove off. He reached into his jeans pocket and came up with a selection of colors and shapes. "You feel ready? You want a little something to get you going?"

They each swallowed a bunch of the brightly colored pills, and maybe then, for the first time, it crossed Benji's mind how far away home was. But his attachment to Vance was visceral. He couldn't think of anyone else. Not even of himself. It was Vance who pulled him up when he was down; it was Vance who brought him down from too high a high. He wore the clothes Vance bought or stole for him. He'd let his hair, taffy-colored with a little gold, grow out, so Vance could fix it the way Vance liked. It was Vance who had bought him a cookbook and started him on the cakes he liked, and who said, "Bet your Mom can't cook as good as you!" And again, it was Vance who taught him some new steps so they could dance in the yard late at night, under the orange and purple lights Benji put up from one cottonwood to another on the house side of the parking lot, who moved him around by the waist, his hand on Benji's shoulder, teaching him the fine points of how to be led.

They were *domestic*. They were a family like any other.

Lennie said, "You're becoming just like a *wife*," and Benji blushed.

However, he had, as his diary showed, moments of *seeing*. He noted, cleaning up after hours, the long shadows of strollers on Houston Street and their encounters. White shirts and dark, narrow trousers, black skirts and gaudy tank-tops met, one or the other lit up a pungent Camel, and a fragment of a face was revealed. Then they went off, together or apart.

Where did they go? Was that what was happening to him?

When Ms. Baldwin stood up in court and said that the two men had "deprived the boy of his innocence", did that mean that Benji hadn't been as anxious to rid himself of that "innocence" as any little girl who dreamt of losing hers?

They strolled the Saturday-night deserted streets downtown in Amarillo and fetched up finally at the YMCA. Benji was thrilled to have Vance's hand on his shoulder and hear Vance say, "This is my kid brother, Benji."

Upstairs in their room, two beds, a dresser, a basin with one small white towel, Vance emptied out his pockets on the dresser. He said he was going to take himself a shower down the hall, but first he split the pills in two, putting Benji's share on the white counterpane of the bed.

Later, Benji met Ron in the cafeteria. Captain Ron is no little girl's dream of losing her cherry, but Vance let on that looks weren't everything, that Ron was part of a world Benji should get used to, the way he had. Besides which, Ron was a hero. If there was damage, it was the war that had done it. And maybe Vance also said, "do it for me."

They took a taxi and went to a party where everyone was on what used to be called a "trip" and no one was what he really was. That was the whole idea. "Look at me," Vance said. "I'm Bette Davis! I'm going to sing for you. This nice black boy has a fine dress for you."

Benji was put into a little red silk dress. He and Ron danced. Grown-ups got these gross ideas and you went along with them, because you had a lot to learn at your age.

Next thing, he was lying on his belly. What happened then hurt, but in the end he accepted it, because in the end pain always stopped. And when it did stop, it felt good to wake up alongside Vance.

That was how Henning saw it.

From the start, he had been struck by the absence of violence in Vance and Lennie. No firearms, no cuts. Everything that happened, when they were two and then when they were three, happened with the apparent consent of the victims. Vance walked willingly, hand on hand, into Lennie's orbit. Together, they closed in on Michael Donnellan of a Sunday morning, and Donnellan hadn't protested when his life was taken over. He must have taken it as his human condition, as what he was. Then Benji had turned up, idling outside the salon; he proved more than willing to go the same route. Right to the very end.

The same way, Henning thought, that children died: with a sense of fatalism, with a minimum of protest. At some point, Benji wrote: "Sometimes I like the things we do together. I don't always like them. Especially Lennie. I don't think he cares about Us."

Just before dawn on the Saturday morning of the Labor Day weekend—school would begin on the Tuesday and Benji and Mary Kay had driven to the supermarket in Big Fork the day before—Mary Kay was still in bed, half awake, when she heard Craig's pick-up coming up the dirt road that ran by the house. Some part of her registered that Craig was back from his Friday night with his "buddies" in Sapphire.

Saturday mornings were always bad mornings.

She had a sense that something was wrong when she heard two doors slam shut on the pick-up, not one. She got up and went to the window of her bedroom. Her window opened onto the barn and what had once been an orchard. The pick-up, a dirty red, stood there, but no Craig.

She wrapped a chenille bathrobe over her shoulders, brushed her hair, and started down the back stairs that led to the kitchen. Then she thought better of it and returned upstairs to look out her window again. A thin, grayish light outlined the barn. There was now a very large man out there. He wore leather leggings and a purple T-shirt. His upper arms were thicker than Christmas hams and covered with tattoos. Then came the part she didn't understand—he was holding something red in his hands.

Then she located Craig, behind the pick-up. He stood there in his familiar morning-after slouch, but he also had a rifle in his hand, the one he kept behind him in the cab of his pick-up. Craig's mouth was apparently shouting, though she couldn't hear him. His rifle was pointed at the big man.

She picked out a third figure on the ground by the side of the track that led to the barn. Nothing clearer than that mop of blond hair, his weekday T-shirt, his tattered denim shorts, his long legs, his sneakers. It was Benji, and he was kneeling, his shoulders were shaking wretchedly.

Not completely awake, Mary Kay tried to work out what was going on. Craig was not quite himself sometimes after Friday nights. He had nightmares, sometimes when he was awake, and it was best if she could get him to their bedroom and he could sleep it off. Chances were he'd been too drunk to drive and some buddy (the big man) had driven him home.

But what was Benji doing up that early? They were supposed to be looking after him at the Salon, the boys.

All she knew was that if something were wrong with him, she had to go down and look after him. She ran down the stairs in her bathrobe and then out the kitchen door toward the barn. "Craig?" she cried out. "Craig? You put that gun down, you hear?"

She saw very clearly the red cloth the big man was carrying. It was a little red dress with thin straps and now she could see the big man was trying to force over Benji's head. "What are you doing to my boy?" she shouted at him. "Craig! What's going on?"

The big man said, "You go back in the house," and Benji looked up at her, the dress round his neck like a thin scarf. *He* didn't want her there. Why wasn't Craig doing anything?

She made no move at all. She couldn't see what she should do. The big man let Benji loose and staggered in her direction. He grabbed her by the arm and started pushing her. "This is between me and Craig and the boy, ma'am," he said. "It'd be better for you if you were in the house."

"You can't do that to my boy!" Where was Craig? And why was Benji still kneeling there a few feet away, doing nothing, not at least running away? "Benji?" she said. "What's going on?"

"'I don't think you understand ma'am. You got no business here."

"Who are you? Craig? Put that gun down. Somebody's going to get hurt." All she could think was, they'd gone by the Salon, they'd picked up Benji. What had they done to the boys, to Lennie and Vance?

"Go back in, Mary Kay," Craig said.

The big man turned round unsteadily and faced Craig. He said, "You got the gun, you know how to use it, use it."

"She won't go, tell her," Craig said, pointing the gun at him. "You tell her what you're doing."

"I didn't know the boy from Adam," the big man said hurriedly. "I don't know you, I didn't know your man 'til last night."

"Tell her," Craig said, and Mary Kay thought, he's not going to *use* the gun, he's not.

"It's a *present*," the big man said. "He left it behind in Amarillo."

"Who did? Left what?" she asked.

"It's his, it's the boy's. I wanted him to have it."

"Tell her *everything*," Craig said.

"I didn't know him. We'd been drinking, taking stuff. I didn't know he was yours, or Craig's here. But the boy I *bought*."

Bought? What kind of a thing was that to say? You didn't buy people. You couldn't go shopping for a Benji. What did he mean? "What do you think you're doing putting that dress on a boy his age?"

Then Craig finally came up alongside them. He said, "You can just shut up now, Ron. It's none of her business. She doesn't understand."

She made a move toward Benji, but he looked up at her, and then at Craig and the big man called Ron. With such hatred, it stopped her cold.

Craig looked at her and said, "He's queer, Mary Kay, I told you he was queer. I done my best for him and for you. You want a queer kid that's your business. I got business of my own in town with those two other queers."

Benji stood up. He took the little red dress from around his neck, slipped it over his head, straightened it out, and walked past all of them to the road, heading towards town.

The sneakers looked out of place.

Chapter nine

When Benji got to the salon that Saturday—it was still early—he found Vance in the kitchen frying up eggs and potatoes. "Where you been? You crazy or something?" Vance asked when he walked in with the red dress on. "You could have got yourself killed. This ain't no fancy-dress place. Go upstairs and take it off."

"I wore it at the party."

"Party's over."

Why didn't grown-ups know what they wanted? They were incomprehensible: they had muscles and guns, but no apparent rules. One day they had sudden rages, on another, exasperating affections. "Captain Ron was at the house. He and Craig nearly got into a fight."

"Do what you're told. Lennie will be down soon. He's not going to be pleased, you taking off last night."

Craig had come by in his red pick-up, only Captain Ron had been driving—as it turned out, on account of Craig sitting on the passenger side with a rifle, his rifle, between his knees. The pick-up's lights had shone right through the apartment upstairs. The lights and the rattle of the diesel had woken Benji up. Craig was sure enough drunk, and in retrospect maybe murderous in intent. No mistaking the way he walked right up the stairs and pushed open the door, finding Benji half sitting up in bed, Vance alongside him, fast asleep. Stuff he couldn't explain to Vance. Vance slept through the whole thing, full of Lennie's pills. He should have said no, when Craig pulled him up and out? Before that came out, better to gain time and talk so Vance couldn't ask that many questions.

"Captain Ron said he 'bought' me. What's that supposed to mean?"

"Frigging Ron. That's where you were? You went off with him last night?"

"This morning. About four, five."

"What did Ron want?"

"Give me a present."

"The dress, huh? He must have the hots for you. Just don't bring it up with Lennie, that's between me and you."

Yes, but what did it mean? "Why shouldn't he know?"

"Because he didn't think it up. Now take that off like I said. We'll have to talk this over, later."

Benji thought back to Craig pointing the gun at Vance in the bed. "He wanted to kill you. I thought he was going to kill me."

"I don't even know him," Vance answered. "Seen him a few times at the Veterans."

"You were there. You left me alone."

"I came back, midnight or so."

The question remained open. "What did he mean, that he 'bought' me? And why wouldn't Lennie like it?"

"Last time I saw you two together, you were dancing with him. I don't know. Maybe they raffled you off. Lots of guys wanted to dance with you. Ron Homolka's a crazy," said Vance. "You don't want to have nothing to do with him."

But, Benji was about to say, you told me what to do, you told me to go off and dance with him. He could tell Vance wasn't happy with what had happened. In fact, it seemed to scare him, so Benji went off upstairs and got out of the dress and got into bed. He was dead tired and fell into a fitful sleep listening to the early-morning noises of Lennie getting up: music on, something from Vienna, his shower beating on the curtain.

The gun came into his dream. Eventually, guns went off.

Craig had held it between his legs all the way back to his house. Then when they got there, Ron had struggled to put the dress over his head. He could feel how the big man wanted him. If Craig hadn't been there, he half-thought and half-dreamed, he would have given Ron what he wanted. If he wanted it that badly. In the end, that was why he'd put the dress on and left them all there to fight it out. He didn't care about the dress, nor what Craig thought of him, or his Mom. He cared about not being under anyone else's control. Being himself. And in his half-sleep he felt happy enough in that dress.

Then he dreamt about the gun again. Craig would come here to the apartment. He would have the gun with him. He woke up, got out of bed, and put the dress back on. He wanted to go down front, into the shop, turn on the bright lights in front of the big mirrors and look at himself. Because in his dream he'd thought he not only looked like a girl, he was one.

Still in the dream, Vance said, "No you can't wear it."

"Why not?"

"Because you're not a girl."

"You mean, if I were a girl, I wouldn't be your friend?"

"I didn't say that. Lennie sees you like that—And I don't say you don't look cute in it—you're not the same kid he started out with."

"I asked about you."

"I do what Lennie says," Vance replied. "You'd better, too."

The last thought Benji had in his dream was that he hadn't done anything *wrong*.

That was when the gun re-entered his dream. And now he didn't dare go down and look at himself. Lennie was about to come out of his room and that much was clear to Benji—that he and Vance did what Lennie said to do. Lennie was cool, but inside him you couldn't tell which way he'd jump.

Could you blame him? Henning wondered. At that age, sex was to boys what grass was to cows; it was what they lived by. The mind that Vance had tilled was rich, fertile soil. As his own had been. He'd been through the whole repertory of Benji's mysterious, ill-defined desires, desires that communicated themselves by touch and smell, by those parts of his body that were more sensitive, by looseness and constriction, by fabrics, in the look of certain necks, hair. He liked talking about them to Benji, and Benji liked talking about them to Vance.

This was all before Labor Day. The summer made for long working days, Monday all the way to Friday night, and Vance missed having the kid around. After work, while it was still light, he walked round town kicking pebbles, scuffing his shoes, peering into shop windows he'd seen a hundred times, peering up sprinklered lawns and into plate-glass picture windows.

It seemed all he ever saw were families. All of these homes contained families. They had a husband, a wife; they contained kids with bedrooms, upper and lower bunks, toys, a TV, carpets on the floor, air-conditioners that whirred, a barbecue out back. Families lived in a special, magical world, protected from feelinglessness. They cared for each other. Mothers yelled out not to cross the street without looking, girls held hands with each other. Some places, at dusk, he caught whole families at their kitchen dinettes, heads bowed, saying grace before eating, as they'd done in his childhood "homes", "Bless us O Lord for these thy gifts." With one foster-family after another.

Henning reckoned that was what Vance was beginning to see: that he needed to belong to someone and have someone belong to him. It was Lennie who didn't want some wide-eyed kid hanging around, asking dumb questions and hanging on his every word, much less Vance's, who was a lot less smart than the boy. So Lennie kidded Vance about Benji, seeing in the boy nothing more than his likeness to a young wife to whom everything about living with someone else is brand new, whom you had to teach how things were. Vance was the not-very-bright husband whose ardor he had to cool down.

But even for Lennie there were incalculables in the boy. First, he allowed himself to be taken away back home by Ron and Craig in the middle of the night, or near enough. Dangerous and stupid. Worse, he himself had taken so damn many tranquillizers he hadn't known about it until morning. And now, a few hours after coming back, here Benji was, apparently having learned nothing about his place in the scheme of things, once again acting as if he were in charge of himself. Making them lunch, guacamole, then a Spanish omelet heavy with potatoes and oil, and then saying with that dumb, innocent face of his, that he was going to slip out for a few minutes and get some stuff he needed for the kitchen. He said, to Vance of course, "If Craig comes, tell him you don't know where I am."

"Sure, Kid," Vance said with a smile.

"Well, I'm only telling you because he was making threats this morning, school starting up on Monday and all."

"If you're telling the truth, he had the chance last night and didn't do nothing. He's just another gutless wonder. And hey, put on some clean clothes."

Lennie didn't say anything, and Benji didn't look his way, but Vance knew Lennie wasn't happy about how things were going. And, as usual, it would turn out to be his, Vance's fault.

Going up Houston Street, Benji kept his eye on the road, expecting any minute to see the red pick-up. He'd been right to be scared of Craig walking into the house with a gun like that, you could never know what a crazy can do, but he wasn't scared of Craig any more. He'd still be sleeping it off. If he saw the red pick-up at all, he was more likely to find his mother resting her head on the wheel, come for a good cry, a hug or something.

Maybe he was like his mother, he thought—unable to get anything right, least of all what others wanted of him. It didn't matter. He'd decided he was going out on his own, was old enough for that, and now he saw no reason, the salon being shut for the holiday weekend, why he shouldn't just stay out as long as he wanted.

It was going past the bank—no familiar red pick-up there, just last-chance Saturday shoppers come into town and hitting the cash machine—that his own mood of change converged with a change in the air around him, as though the air were agreeing with him, doing something to him too, giving him a surge of power.

A shadow fell on him and he looked up to see a single cloud, the color of old slate, slanting across the sky. Two blocks later, half way to the church, that one cloud was signing up others. He walked along more freely now, long arm swinging by his side. Then someone on the far side of the street called out "Hi Benji!" in a friendly manner, and he stopped. But he didn't see who it was.

He kept on going until he was clear through the main part of town and the light started collapsing in front of him, pushed down under clouds so that wires and telegraph poles, roofs and big cottonwoods, stood out, lit only on their far sides.

A few blocks behind, the same clouds marched, flat and silent, over Vance, whose light-heartedness was gone, and who had said to Lennie just a few moments before, "I'd better see what the Kid's getting up to." Because Benji had said something about Craig and a gun but he hadn't been paying attention, which had made Lennie sore.

"Spare the rod and spoil the child," Lennie had grinned.

As so often, Vance didn't really catch his drift. Only that Lennie was sore. Vance couldn't even explain his own anxiety, though he had moments like that often enough: this feeling that he'd made a bad mistake but didn't know what it was. He never felt like that when *he* was threatened, when a cop drove by, when somebody pulled in for gas and he had his toy pistol at an old man's back, by the register. He felt it when someone else was threatened. In this case a very young wife he also had to protect.

Benji, who had reached Dairy Queen on the far edge of town, stood at the mosquito-screened door. He had ordered a chili dog and a Dr. Pepper when he saw, on the opposite side, where the Mexican shacks tumbled down towards the gully, Captain Ron coming down his way, legs more than a little apart as though he had a medicine ball between his knees. Only this Captain Ron was no longer a fearsome figure. He looked something like an overstuffed papier-mâché figure fallen off a flatbed during a parade.

When the big man was level with him, Benji stepped out from the shade and said, "Over here, Captain Ron. I'm over here."

The big man waited carefully for the cars passing by and then picked his way across the street. When he got by his side, Benji could see his leggings were cracked and patched at the knee, and his leather jacket sprouted its lining, a weed of golden silk. This new Ron, bashfully looking at his feet, said, "I was just coming looking for you. I wanted to say I was sorry."

"For what?"

"For the dress. It wasn't my idea, it was your Dad's idea."

"He's not my father."

"Your step-father's, then."

"He's not my step-father."

"Okay, the man who lives with your mother."

"She's not my mother."

"Let's sit down. Can you buy me a Coke or something? I'm broke."

The boy who told Henning this, a high school junior who worked there weekends, remembered how clear and blue and violet Benji's eyes were. Not much else.

They took the dogs and drinks and sat down in back under a plastic umbrella and the radio in the Dairy Queen kitchen squawked with static, a Rangers game on. An out-of-state car drove up and the driver yelled out something about if there was a hospital nearby, his wife in back was feeling poorly.

Suddenly clear, the radio broke into the game and said storms were expected throughout North Texas and especially Nava and Rio Seco counties.

Paying no heed to what was being said out front, and knowing the nearest hospital was back in the direction the car had been coming from, Benji leaned forward across the plastic table and said to Ron, "Are you queer? What's it mean, being queer?"

Not that he really didn't know, but because he thought bringing it out into the open would put him on more even terms with

Captain Ron. Also, as he told Vance later, because the smell of Ron, even outdoors, even in the fresh, cooler air of the front moving in, that smell of dissatisfaction, of a lousy digestion, of junk food and carbonated beverages, had taken him straight back to Amarillo. And this time he was going to look Ron right in the eyes.

Half of his dog broke off in Ron's big hand. Picking it up and stuffing it into his mouth, he said: "Queer's not good. You'll see. Yeah, I'm queer. If you're a girl you don't like boys; if you're a boy you don't like girls."

"In Amarillo, those were all queers?"

"Hey listen, Kid, Vance said you were small for your age, but he said you were sixteen. After, he told me you weren't."

"Vance is my friend."

"I know that."

"You knew him before?"

"I guess."

"You want another dog?"

"How'm I going to get out of here? I came here to explain to you and to tell Vance not to worry about you-know-who. He's got a broken arm. I broke it for him."

"And Mom?" Benji reached into his jeans and came out with a bill neatly folded in sixteen. "I got ten dollars, if that'll help."

"I walked here. She said she had to look after her guy."

"His name's Craig Lofter."

"She said for you to go home. She doesn't know anything about Amarillo, honest. It was Vance bragging about it at the vFW that started the whole thing. Craig got mad."

"Bragging about what?"

"Me and you."

"You and me what?"

"It's not good. I don't want to talk about it. I didn't know what I was doing. Those guys had cocaine and stuff. I'm just sorry. You're a good kid."

As he was hesitating, Benji put the bill on Ron's plate. "Take it," he said. "It'll get you somewhere. I can get you more at the shop. Vance will give you some."

"I'm not going there now. I was going to tell you, so you could tell Vance. I'm getting out of this place. I really like you, which is why I'm telling you, you ought to blow off that Vance. Him and Lennie."

"I told you, Vance is my friend."

"You don't know what he's really like."

"I like him anyway. Could be I'm queer like Craig says. I'm a lot happier with Vance than I am at home."

"You can't know if you are or you aren't. But guys can want you even if you're not. Queer. Vance is queer. In jail he was called 'Jail Mary.' On account of he was always falling on his knees and opening his mouth."

"And what?"

"What do you think?"

"He was in jail?"

"He was."

Benji considered the idea of Vance being in jail. It didn't bother him much. He asked, Lennie in jail?"

"Not yet. Not that I know of. Lennie gets others to do his stuff for him."

Benji tried to think, but just then dust lifted on the street as a wind blew in. The plastic umbrella over their table rattled and the boy in a white cap with meshing for the air to come in (the young man Henning talked to) came rushing out from the kitchen to start putting things away: hadn't they noticed there was a storm brewing?

"He had a lot of trouble with the nuns," Captain Ron said, ignoring the wind and their paper plates flying. "He's never forced you to do things with him?"

Benji tried not to, but he blushed. He didn't want to talk about himself and Vance. That was private stuff. They cuddled; he more or less let Vance do what he wanted, which made him feel good. He said: "He doesn't have to *force* me."

Rain spattered on the plastic shingles of Dairy Maid. Tires began to make a swish as their drivers hurried home to look after things they'd left outside. Benji had the feeling nothing that was going on around them would bother the big man: he wanted company. They could get wet forever as long as he had someone to talk to.

"He *hated* those nuns, you know. Must have been about your age when he was with them. Set fire to their habits, pissed in the sacristy, tried to climb up on one of them on a picnic for the boys, while she was off gathering wood for the campfire, a Sister! They had to send him away."

Benji knew Captain Ron was giving him a warning, only Benji didn't really want to hear. He felt sorry for the big man. He was such a mess.

Vance, hiding from the rain under the portico of the church where Benji had sung and Lennie had first spotted him, watched them from maybe a hundred-and-fifty yards away: watched the big man with his bulging arms on the table and his hands tangling with his beard and mouth; watched the Kid talking earnestly, slight enough to get blown away, but talking like a grown-up, holding his ground; watched, he thought, with a stir of excitement, as though he were Lennie, waiting to see what would happen.

It began to rain hard, the kid in the white hat had taken all the umbrellas back in, and still the two of them sat at their picnic table, getting soaked and talking. The sight of them up the road reminded Vance of the party, of what a star the boy had been with his clean looks and his fancy vocabulary, polite to everyone. He could've hustled a mint.

Unfortunately, it was like Lennie said, Vance thought: kids didn't last, suddenly they sprouted hair and wings to take off with.

"Break them in," Lennie said. "Only don't you touch him until I say so."

So Vance had thought of Ron. Some real meat, he said, getting excited talking about it to Lennie, two hundred fifty, seventy-five, on top of him, that would teach the kid who was boss, give him the feel for it. "What do you think?" he asked, mentioning Ron.

But Ron had been a bust. And Lennie had predicted that, too. He said Ron hadn't got two nickels to rub together, which at his age was a crying shame. Look at his situation, Lennie said. Ron was an occasional dealer, okay, but his few customers (all chance buyers, late-night girl addicts, kids fresh out of correctional camps and without contacts, and bikers who briefly took him for one of their own) were a long way away. Even in California he wasn't making out, wasn't making any real money. And what happened when he flubbed? When his sexual apparatus wouldn't respond or his revolver wouldn't fire?

"Who else?" Vance had said. "I can't just throw the kid to the wolves."

Lennie said: "And why not?"

Vance guessed that was why he had that feeling he'd made a dumb mistake by going ahead with Ron. As he didn't want to make another one, he tried to play it like Lennie. He stayed at a distance and watched.

By then, the light from under the clouds ran like a clear stream along the highway and, as in the hymn Benji liked particularly, where the truth is like that light, it carried a certain reproach Captain Ron's way. He wasn't getting his story across. Nor his desire. The big man buried his massive head up to his ears in his leather jacket and began to wonder, looking furtively that way, if this storm, still only distant thunder and lightning as horizontal as the band of reds and violets under the setting sun, were not God talking to him, telling him that once in his life he ought to go for what he wanted.

The Kid was shivering and Ron got up and walked round the table to give him a big hug and some of his excess warmth; but Benji wriggled free and stood, soaked, a few feet away from Ron's outstretched and shiny leathered arms.

All of which Vance saw from his vantage point, nice and dry thank you very much, thinking the number of ways in which he could make Ron really suffer.

However, the illumination that had come into Ron's mind from that brief contact with the boy's body was not something new. After the party, seeing the red dress left behind, he hadn't been able to drive the boy from his mind. In his wild dreams, which included war and wet, warm friendships with the young, he concocted a scheme in which he would ride off into the sunset (actually sunrise, since it was a lot safer for him to go back East than out to California) with Benji in tow. Benji's thumb out on the highway for hitchhiking. He reckoned that if he could somehow last a week or so, and Benji could accept him as a friend, maybe even a lover, he could make the boy truly scared of Vance and Lennie, by going into details he knew intimately. At which point, having *befriended* the boy, taken him off somewhere, enjoyed him, hidden him away, he might even pull it off, take the boy back to California, pass him off as his son. If friendship wasn't what the boy wanted and needed, why was he still standing there, hands on his hips, rain dropping down the freckles on his cute snub nose?

He tried again, but again Benji backed off. Just as Ron shrugged and said, "Come on, Kid, let's get out of here before we drown," Vance emerged from the church portico across the street.

Captain Ron was the first to see him. Trying to be cool. With that swagger of his, which was both sinuous and cocky.

"Hi there, Ron," Vance said, holding out his hand. "And look what we've got here! Young Benji!" He swiveled lightly and put his hand on Benji's shoulder. He said, "Lennie's been worrying about you. Don't you think it's time you got back to the Sa-LON? Also, your Mum called, I have no idea why, you being quite fit and all to walk round town by yourself and meet up with whoever you like."

Ron's swallowed up Vance's hand. "I was on my way in to tell you 'bout your buddy Craig, he's got a gun…"

"Yeah, I heard." Vance turned back to Benji. "Well, young feller, what you waiting for? Captain Ron and I have a few words to say to each other. Ron here wants to be getting on his way, don't you, Ron?"

"I ain't got no money, Vance. You know that. Apart ten bucks the boy here gave me."

"A kind kid. Get cracking, boy. Just because we're shut for the weekend don't mean there's nothing to do back there."

Benji turned his back on both of them and started off running to beat the rain, his sneakers slapping the sidewalk. Maybe he'd go back to the Hair Today; maybe he'd just keep going.

Vance said, "You don't need money, Ron. You got two feet. Besides which it happens maybe I'm going the same way you're going. I feel the need for some action. It's boring in a little place like this. And you can let go my goddam hand now, Ron. We ain't on a date or nothing."

"Where you going?"

"That matter? You can't stay here. Least not hanging round the Dairy Queen. Sheriff hears you been hanging 'bout Mary Kay's boy, Craig's not the only one's going to come looking for you."

"I broke Craig's arm."

"Well, good for you!"

Seeing his dream of Benji blowing away, the heart of the storm stamping up on them with heavy legs that touched the prairie, the rain coming, Ron made a last try to resist. "Why would the Sheriff come for me and not for you, Vance.? It's you took the boy up."

"Maybe Lennie told him about you. See what I mean? I'm going back to get the car and make sure Benji's okay. I'll pick you up front of the bank. You be there."

Chapter ten

The storm came and went. All Saturday night, Benji waited. But Vance didn't come back. There was nobody at home (Mary Kay had taken Craig to Big Fork to get his arm fixed), so Benji couldn't go anywhere, and Lennie, having switched from Vienna to the South Pacific, stayed in his room. So did Benji, propped up in the double bed, writing in his diary, a book with a clasp and a key, that gave every day an inch.

The entries weren't so much what was happening, but a bunch of "subjects." Henning read in the sheaf of Xeroxes about "the mirror game," the "wet bed," about "tools".

There was still a big pier mirror in the room Benji shared with Vance. They stood naked before it—either holding hands or with Vance's arm around Benji's shoulder. They were aware that Lennie stood in the doorway behind them, and was watching.

Benji watched Vance's hand at work. All he had to do was stand there and look down. Vance said he'd be able to do it soon himself.

When Benji woke up after Vance's nocturnal rubbings, he found his side of the bed and his thighs wet.

Things like that.

Around nine the next morning, which was Sunday—Benji was getting ready to go to choir practice—he heard Lennie's old Subaru pull into the back of the house. Lennie beat Benji to the back window in Vance's room. He was that anxious. Because when Vance took off anywhere, who knew what would happen, or if he'd come back.

First Vance's left leg came out of the car. It was bloody. So were his shirt, his sneakers. So was his hand on the door-handle.

Lennie ran downstairs and out back onto the porch: "Jesus! What happened to you? Where've you been?"

Vance walked unsteadily right past him toward the house. Benji hovered at the head of the stairs. Lennie put out an arm to stop Vance. Vance shook free of the arm. He said, "Lay off, will you?"

"I'm talking to you," Lennie shouted after him. "You've been out all night. What the hell have you been doing?"

"Fuck you," said Vance. "I don't owe you any explanations. And don't shout at me, all right?"

"I need to know what you've done. You're putting both of us at risk. You know that."

Vance went past him toward the kitchen, with Benji alongside him. "Where'd you go? I waited here the whole night."

"I went for a little ride, that's all."

Putting coffee on the stove, Benji said, "If you take all that stuff off, I can put it in the machine. You have a fight with Captain Ron?"

"That creep?" Lennie asked, coming in behind them. "What's the matter with you. Some dumb thing like you do every time you're left to think for yourself, and now we're wiped out? He's trouble."

"Not no more, he ain't. Calm down," said Vance. "Ron won't bother us."

"Oh, great! You say he won't bother us. Is that blood yours or his?"

"Bit of both."

"You *kill* him?"

"What you think?"

"You took *my* car. Your friends at the VFW will remember the guy."

Vance looked up at Lennie in a way Benji had never seen before; as if he were challenging him. "You want to run, you run. I've had it up to here with your don't-get-into-trouble routine."

"You killed him, didn't you? What did you use? A knife? You leave it there, throw it away? What? Where's Ron? Where did all this go on?"

"Down South a ways."

"Off the highway?"

"Sure we were off the highway..."

Lennie went back out to inspect the car. He came back in, furious. "There's blood on the front seat."

Vance gave him that look again. "It's an old car, Lennie. Who cares if it's got blood on the seat. Maybe you've been having your frigging period."

"Here's some coffee," said Benji, putting the blue enamel cup down in front of Vance. "Can I get you some, Lennie?"

Lennie said, "You can get your ass over to choir. I got serious business here."

Meanwhile Vance sipped at his coffee. "You didn't kill him, did you?"

Vance smiled and Lennie sat down across the table from him. Benji gave him his cup.

"All I said was, he wouldn't bother us. That's what I meant and that's what I said."

"Where is he?"

"Somewhere down Route 207, Palo Duro..."

"Can you see him from the road?"

"Shit, nothing else but rock and hard ground that way."

"I said, can you see him?" Lennie was taking charge again. Those peculiar, predator's eyes, worked on Vance.

"Not unless he got up and he's hitching a ride, and I don't think that's likely. All I did was beat him up a little. Don't see him stopping a truck the way he looked. Not with his record."

But even Benji knew that something had shifted. Lennie had the kind of cold, hard self-mastery that made him walk away from Vance, just telling him to get himself cleaned up, but the tension between Vance and Lennie was now out in the open.

And, Henning thought, the spell had been broken. Now, for the first time there had been violence. It had been inevitable.

But like the storm, it blew over. Vance and Lennie were tied to each other; each of them knew that.

Come Labor Day Monday, Vance thought they were back to the good old days before they ever hit this creepy little town. Nice and early, not telling the Kid, who was asleep, Lennie said, "Let's go for a ride."

Great! A beer in hand, Vance squeezed himself into the Subaru's passenger seat, no idea where they were going; then Lennie, checking out the crease in his chinos before starting up the car. Heading East and then South out of town, slow as ever, the sun barely up but shining in their eyes, a thin frost on the windshield: "What the hell time is it anyway?" Vance asked.

Lennie lit a cigarette and the sun came up further, uneventful.

Soon enough, going through rock and scrub, past forlorn cafes and gas stations, Vance thought it probably wasn't going to be like the good old days, no matter that he was in a good mood and free, out on the open road, which was where they were best together. Wherever they were going, it wasn't going to be far, and they'd end up driving back to Sapphire. Apart from the boy, he was sick of the place. And sometimes sick of the boy, too. He didn't want anyone clinging to him.

Lennie was tense. After they'd stopped for breakfast and got down Route 207 where Vance said he'd been with Ron, twice Lennie got out of the car and walked out into the waste, looking all round him before taking a leak. Each time he was even more jittery when he got back in the car. He kept on asking Vance, "Is this more or less where?" and Vance would say it wasn't. Lennie said it all looked alike to him. "I don't believe you came this way at all."

"Then why you bothering?"

When Vance began to recognize the butte on the right, prob-ably ten miles away in a haze, and a disused billboard they'd passed a mile back, and came up to the place where Vance had pushed Captain Ron out of the car, Vance wanted to let Lennie drive right past it. Maybe claim he couldn't remember. Instead, he put his hand on Lennie's arm and said: "Someplace like this. This stretch."

From then on, Lennie drove even more slowly and stopped every place there was a human being to ask if they'd seen this big guy, six feet plus, fat, all leathers, long, greasy hair, you know, a biker.

After a half-hour like that Lennie turned the car around and headed back North. "You killed him, didn't you? If I keep looking for him, am I going to find him somewhere—road-kill?"

"You're not going to find him. Let's get back."

"After the Kid we go."

"After the Kid what, we go?"

"After you get to do everything to him you ever imagined. The ultimate ball. I'm sick of hairdressing."

That made both of them laugh.

Henning's guess was that Vance took Ron a long way off from the highway and put him under rocks in some arroyo. That would have been work, not fun.

For fun he had Lennie.

That night, when they got back to Sapphire, Lennie went up to his room and put on some music. Downstairs, Vance sat with Benji on the back porch, on another cold, clear night, one on which the stars would be big and bright. Some of the time they held hands; some, distended, they spent watching football. Or Vance did, because Benji read a Willa Cather Mrs. Spenser had recommended. Occa-sionally, through the noise of the commercials, they heard Lennie's typewriter upstairs, the one that he'd brought home from this year's auction night for cheerleaders. It was a normal sound. Lennie liked to keep his thoughts in good, clear form.

When Benji had gone up to bed, Vance heard Lennie's door open and the sound of his steps coming down the stairs. Vance hadn't been thinking of Benji at all, but rather about getting out of there. And he hadn't been thinking of Lennie either, but rather that once out of there he could split and be on his own.

It was that Sunday night that Lennie handed Vance his instructions, neatly typed. One of Lennie's lists. The numbered list Vance was going to tape to the wall of his room, by the light switch.

Chapter eleven

S itting opposite Henning in his orange prison jump suit with a zip up the front, Lennie shone like the fruit on a tree. Bright sunlight through the wire mesh between, picked out on him the authentic pockmarks of an orange. Above his jump suit, his face was scrubbed, young and refreshed: morally and physically. This was a new phase in his life—no reason that it shouldn't be even better than the last.

The raw material of his pleasure was all about him: encounters, play, power, alliances. This was a group no different from other groups: Hal's semi-scouts, the grunts in Guam. Among the many you could ply your private way.

One rule Lennie established on arrival. Led off to his cell after the formalities by a young man, new to the job, who, meaning to be friendly, put his hand on Lennie's arm to guide him, Lennie said, "No one touches me." He said it so fiercely, so apart, that the young guard backed off right away.

Each time Henning went to see him, each time more so, Lennie made him feel that these surroundings—the visiting room, the antiseptic cream-colored walls, the partitions with mesh in the glass, the hard chairs, the phallic mikes—put Lennie in a commanding position. On Henning's side of the glass sat a fifty-something, non-descript man with nicotine-stained fingers and poor teeth. He wore a crumpled seersucker suit, he had receding hair that might once have been blond, and he wanted something from Lennie, who was, by contrast, in the prime of life, fit, muscular, charming, and cool, and eager to offer up his versions of the truth.

Henning was made to feel he was already in the shadow-world. Lennie was lit bright. Each time Henning liked visiting less and stayed more briefly. He particularly resented having to listen to Lennie's "philosophy", half-baked ideas culled from the books he'd half-read in college.

The precarious hold Henning had on Lennie (far greater than that he held over Vance, who showed up to talk only because it broke up the boring routine) was that Lennie was curious about him, think-ing about Henning as his aspirant biographer.

Death, Lennie might say, was the most interesting thing there was. Death of any kind, even the Little Deaths of his many ejacula-tions. But surely Henning agreed that the Big One was the ultimate experience: "Each time I can feel it closer and closer; the closer it gets, the more exciting it is."

Uh-huh.

It wasn't that Lennie was lying, but that all his truths were self-serving; they gave him bragging rights over a large chunk of human experience. For instance, Lennie wasn't about to die. It was others who had died or been destroyed. But by talking about death like that, in general terms, he skipped romantically through the deaths particular to him.

Obviously, the only important, sexy death for Lennie was his own. The others barely counted. Only his own was attractive. And if you studied Lennie's life, the progression of this idea in his mind was logical. Young Lennie had been surprised by his reaction to the pain of others, animal or human. From there on he'd gone out in search of those things that gave him the biggest kicks. Until finally, touching up against death, the Big One, he had begun to create them himself. That was his résumé. That was his ambition.

"You wrote me you knew 'all about' Guam," Lennie said on one of Henning's last visits. "I doubt that. Not *everything*."

Henning said he'd only just finished reading the transcript of the court martial. "Is there more to it?"

"Some said I raised the fire."

"Did you?"

Lennie couldn't help himself. He had to be a smart-ass. He said, "If you don't know that, you don't know everything."

Henning didn't know everything, Lennie was right. What he did know was bad enough. But the source of Lennie's power lay in what Henning didn't know. Thus Lennie could raise the stakes, visit after visit. All he had to say was, "You don't know *everything*."

The power Lennie had, was the power that comes with being indifferent to others, living or dead.

His mother had called him out of the garden where he was hiding, but he didn't know where he was. Because he lived in a world of pure sensation. Only what *he* felt mattered.

Whereas Henning was fatally condemned to seeing what he imagined. If he'd been the one in the pen, and Lennie his examiner, Henning would have been forced to admit that his dreams were full of self-accusations: all pronounced by people who obviously know him far better than he knew himself. Every excrescence of character, every failure of nerve, had been excoriated countless times. The texts he saw on bad nights were derisive reviews of himself. They listed all his failures, going back to Original Sin. But above all they dwelled patiently and consistently on his dead son, Luca. Why else would Benji have interested him? Since the two boys might once have been the same age.

Lennie grinned fiercely when he said, "You can only imagine what you don't know, so why would you want to write about me when you don't even know what I think or feel?" Then he tilted back his chair, out of reach of the mike so that his voice came through on Henning's side as if from a great distance, and added: "Oh, we have consciences to examine, you and I." Then, matter-of-fact again, he said, "You don't know, do you? You don't know about you, so how can you know about me?"

It wasn't much of an answer for Henning to say he could supply what was wanting.

Once he'd read through the transcript of Lennie's court martial, there were certain things he could imagine vividly; he could even track, with some probability, what Lennie had been thinking and doing—always wondering what a court of field-grade officers (with crew-cuts and families) might have been thinking. Who, for want of proof or an over act, dealt with an abomination with a mere discharge.

Henning spent hours on the transcripts, but never shook off his own sense of what it must have been like. And what it had been like was way beyond anything he could cope with. It belonged in that very large category that consisted of thoughts he could not have and acts he could not perform.

Added to that, as Henning well knew, was Lennie's freakish sensibility: often morally dead, but often deadly when perceiving weakness in others.

He'd put the damned transcript away, have a coffee at Maggie's, read the day-old papers that lay on the tables, and rub his eyes as though that would drive the pictures away. Pictures Henning knew, and Lennie knew, involved some of the deepest of Henning's own fears: of death in any form, but of death by fire especially.

Going back to his motel room and the foot-high (with appendices) transcript, he saw the connection to Hope's death clearly enough: the ultimate killer as bystander, the watcher of cats who played with birds as of Hope and her bike sinking sleekly in the turmoil of the Mississippi.

He said to himself that there must have been dozens if not hundreds of such incidents in Lennie's life that never had and never would show up. Each of them incremental, each leading up to Benji.

Three semesters doing pre-med at Stanford: good grades and no disciplinary problems. Did Lennie want to talk about that? No, he was more intent on his credentials as an intellectual who read Nietzsche and Schopenhauer, the sweet voices of nihilism and despair that Henning had listened to himself. Though the one thing he seemed to have studied at Stanford was pharmacology.

What did Lennie talk about? His mother driving him down from Washington to Palo Alto and helping him decorate his room (pennants on his wall and a second-hand carpet on the floor). Henning didn't think it could have been *that* exciting.

Yet this bright and perverse nineteen-year-old drifter hadn't gone to Stanford until Davenport, Iowa's Police Department started asking difficult questions. And after three semesters, all of twenty-two, he enlisted, walking in off the street on the first of January. Had something else Henning didn't know about caught up with Lennie?

If so, it had been, like his army service, of no interest to the Nava County District Attorney's office.

Two years later, he was back home with his parents and a dishonorable discharge for "dereliction of duty." According to Jon Eastling, Lennie's attorney, his stay at home had been sheer garbage-time. He had taken no job that Henning could discover, had had no interests, had done nothing wrong. Henning doubted he had been brooding. No one said anything about drugs, Lennie had no record, but that was what Henning suspected. He was holed up with needles.

Guam had been horrible.

Four Blacks had screamed like horses trapped in a barn-fire and died while Lennie had been standing behind a row of palms barely thirty feet away.

Henning knew what Lennie had been doing. He was indifferent. His hands were in his pockets, busy like ferrets, but slow and stealthy as cats.

"You heard them," he said to Lennie one day, wanting to shock him out of complacency. "You smelled them. They saw you."

Lennie grinned back at him. "You're excited, Mr. Forsell. It gives you a kick, doesn't it? Which is it that gets to you, the dying or the fire? You'd like to read my mind?"

The duty, the dereliction, had been sentry duty the night the fire broke out in the guardhouse attached to the MP barracks. On the Saturday night in question the guardhouse had contained nine prisoners. One was a second lieutenant sent there to "cool off" after a brawl in a beach bar, but by ten that night he'd been confined to quarters instead. Of the others, three were whites on weekend confinement for drunkenness; one was a Chinese civilian who'd tried to break into the nurses' quarters. The other four were black, and it was not established at the court martial whether the fact that they were all confined in one cell, away from the other prisoners, came about by their own choice.

The guard-house was built of brick, but an extension had been built onto one end of it that was made of wood on the outside, sheet rock and plaster inside, and regulation metal doors and bars: "more solid than it sounds," said the Provost of the base in his testimony. "Without tools I don't think the men could have broken out." It was in that extension that the four Blacks were held, and in their cell that a fire broke out at 1.44 A.M., at the time that Lennie was on sentry duty on the perimeter fence.

The Sergeant on duty that hot, sticky night, Sgt. Culpeper, testified that he had made his rounds of the cells, checked that the prisoners were all sound asleep, and only stepped outside a few minutes to check up on a noise he heard in the palm grove that lay between the guard-house and the beach, thinking it might be Chinese trying to get "the prisoner Lo out, tensions between the army and the civilian population being at a high level."

Sergeant Culpeper testified that he had found no one in the grove ("Not even the defendant?" asked the presiding officer. "No Sir. I thought he must have been on the far side.") and was turning back when he heard what sounded like an explosion, and next thing he knew, that whole end of the barracks was a blaze.

But Lennie was there. He was in the grove just past the perimeter fence, a fact that was established by his footprints and by a half-dozen cigarette butts, plus (more deadly evidence) a small toilet kit bag containing "medicines", one of which was a painkiller prescribed for Lennie by name.

It came down to a matter of time. Had Lennie been there when the fire broke out? And if so, why did he not immediately raise the alarm?

It was agreed that given the nature of the fire—its suddenness, the barred cellblock—there was no possibility that the prisoners could have been released in time except by someone with the key to their cell. Sergeant Culpeper had such a key. But by the time he reached the barracks, the fire barred his way to the cell door. He did what he could, releasing the other four prisoners only just in time, and as the fire-truck arrived.

The four Blacks in the MP barracks, two of them gripping the bars on the window, the way their charred bodies were found, must have seen Lennie. He wasn't far away and he was illuminated by flames that lit up the palms from top to bottom. They danced, yelled, screamed and wept, but Lennie didn't move. By then the fire had reached the roof and flames licked along the outside wall.

Henning held the photographs of the end results. Not what Lennie must have seen: their gestures, their hands now riveted to the bars, melted to them, skin coming off in strips. That part of the jailhouse went with a bang, then a whoosh, and finally a roar. As Culpeper was running back. He had a few hundred yards to run, at full tilt. Meaning that it was all over in three, four minutes.

Lennie must have been rooted to the spot, unable to move until his release came. Then there would be blissful calm and his brain would be lucid.

He was found peacefully asleep at the foot of the palm.

"Did you raise the fire?" Henning asked.

He might as well have asked if Lennie had stepped out on the levee in the dark and so scared Hope that she had steered her bike straight into the drink. Such details were just circumstances to Lennie. Snails get crushed in their shells, four Blacks were so tightly wrapped in flames, all they could do was rise as sparks or fall as carbon. In Lennie's world, Henning realized, the beloved never fled.

An elementary anger had Henning by the throat. "You liked it that they were helpless, isn't that it?" He thought of the Number

One boy imprisoned by Hal's hands, Hal's view confined to the top of the scalped head below him, or Hope being found taped to their bed in a Davenport motel.

"Don't you think freedom is an overrated business?" asked Lennie. "Someone touches you, that binds you to them."

Henning remembered what Vance had said at the trial: it wasn't just *any* duct tape that had been used on Benji, it was the best. Lennie was always a perfectionist, and in his world, "binding" took on a new meaning.

Lennie didn't even blink. You could talk about tape and remind him Benji was just a child; nothing was to be allowed to penetrate Lennie's inner world.

That day, Lennie's parting shot was: "You do fancy me, don't you."

Did he fancy him? At all? Never?

Propped up before Henning was a photograph of his only son, Luca. He had no children because he no longer had that son.

In the photograph, his son was Benji's age.

Henning saw in Luca's eyes, in the slight pout of his lips, the aggressive tilt of his slight jaw (why deny it?), that same pluck and over-confidence with which Benji must have viewed Lennie. Luca, too, had been conscious of his omnipotence. He had been charming and courted. Adults liked to touch him, to watch him smile, to run their hands through his hair. They admired his entirety, his sense of the future, of what he was going to be, what he wanted.

Henning was glad Luca would never read about Lennie and Vance and Benji. And Henning wished, in a complicated way, that neither Luca nor Benji had ever existed, who had childhoods from which, as from a chrysalis, their butterfly emerged. It was better for children not to know Evil. And, contrary to what Lennie believed, the so-called "thrill" of Evil had no attraction for Henning. Save that primordial curiosity as to how it entered the human mind.

Chapter twelve

T he idea always was, Vance testified, that the people Lennie picked out should be made helpless, become simple possessions, like tools which could be used for many purposes. Did he include himself amongst those? Or was it his lawyer's idea to make Vance yet another of Lennie's victims?

At least that was how the argument started out. Benji as the apprentice. A boy looking for a way to be vicariously an adult, just by hanging around with one, as though that made it possible for him to share all the secrets adults kept from kids. The kid swept up, helped out. Lennie only tolerated him, kids being a nuisance.

But then Benji took hold. Like prairie grass. He had no other place to put down roots in. He took to the clothes, he took to the talk; he was unobtrusive, polite. So there was some affectionate necking, a little play, a bit of sentiment, for Vance could see his young self in Benji. "I never said I wasn't fond of him. We hung out together, we had some good times. But there wasn't any *intention*."

You mean, Henning said to himself, as Vance wasn't there to

have it flung at him, there were typed-out instructions on the wall but really Vance had been just "fooling around," and the whole thing was just an accident. Benji was an accident. There were hundreds of Benjis wandering around alone, aimless, with sneakers on their feet and a skateboard under their arms, lonely kids more than ready to be a grown-up's pal. But in Sapphire? Where kids went round in packs—or as Lennie, that sociopath said, where the locals were "fully socialized"? Here Benji was unique. Vance said, "The Kid thought we were cool."

Did Vance even know what the truth was?

Cool? Henning said to Lennie, "I guess he didn't know where becoming cool would take him, huh?"

Lennie waved his hand at that. "The Kid was infatuated. He thought maybe we'd take him on the road with us, the way some kids want to run away with a circus. What kind of a life did the Kid have, anyway? Books and a Mom who never said boo to her guy?"

With Vance, Lennie explained, you just looked for the simplest explanation. Take him or leave him the way he was. He said, "As far as I can tell, he's *always* had sticky fingers. Bodies and buns, skin, hair, silk and stuff. He was that way in jail, I heard. It doesn't matter to him whose body: nuns, hairdressers, beatniks, even cops, it doesn't matter. Vance doesn't *think*. He just does what comes naturally to him."

Meanwhile, Lennie told him how the world was. At least the way Lennie saw how the world was. But Lennie's world wasn't operable without an instrument of some kind. As Henning said to Lennie, "I couldn't invent a more perfect solipsist than you. But you've got a flaw, haven't you. You need someone else to give you your kicks."

"He was useable, if that's what you mean."

No, what Henning meant was that Lennie needed Vance to do all the things he wouldn't or couldn't do. There'd always been someone in that role: his mother, Hal, prisoners on Guam, Hope. A set of eternal triangulations! And how perfectly adapted to the role Vance was! A limited language, powerful hatreds, soft bowels, weak knees. When Lennie spotted a mark and said to Vance, that one's for you, Vance described it as "like the nuns giving you a whole afternoon off, wow!"

Henning didn't get much out of Vance. That he'd been manipulated by Lennie didn't bother him one bit; he *liked* being manipulated. He asked Vance about the letters Lennie had written him in jail, the *love*-letters.

Vance laughed at Henning. "If you think that, they'd open your eyes." He laughed for some while.

As long as the scenery changed all the time, Vance was okay, and sometimes you did things that were really *bad* just to change the scenery. All the original Bolsheviks, a word he couldn't get quite right, confessed they were finks and spies and worthless shit. Not only were they worthless shit, but so were their wives and their mothers. Why'd they do a thing like that? Because even being shot was a change of scenery.

That's what jail was like, Vance said, and in a lot of ways he'd rather be dead.

Talking about the last month (September) before the 911 call, Vance said his job was to explain the facts of life to Benji. He prepped the boy: "Like they shave you before the chair or an operation, or you peel potatoes before you cook."

It was a new stage in Benji's life "You got a cute ass, someone's going to use it." It was a new stage in Vance's life too. Doing "what comes naturally to him," Lennie had said. "Of course Vance lusted after the Kid. I held him off for a long time."

"But then you said 'go ahead.' You wrote out what, where, how often, how."

Vance sang (in another borrowed voice—Barbara Stanwyck's?) what sounded like a hymn-tune, "Washed in the blood of the Lamb, washed in the blood of the Lamb."

Meanwhile, he put panty hose over the Kid's head, wrapped a little rope round him and tied him up to a hook in back of the closet. "Now you know what it feels like when what you want's not what someone else wants. If someone wants to tie you up or cut you

123

up or stick it to you, nothing you think or feel or yell about is going to work, he's going to do it."

The Kid would beg him to let him out, cut him down, he couldn't breathe, you name it.

"I think you're not getting my message," Vance said. "It's what *we* want that counts, not what *you* want. Remember what that guy on the moon said, he was going where no man had gone before. That's you. You're going where you never been before."

He was talking about the boy's ass.

No wonder Ms. Baldwin had taken a long, cleansing shower after putting stuff like that to a Nava County jury. For God's sake, a child's ass was not an independent piece of flesh. Presumably it had some connection to his soul.

"That's enough for today," Henning said.

"You think I forced him? He came back week after week, didn't he? You don't like what I'm telling you, do you? That it turned him on and he came back for more? Nobody forced him to turn up every Friday."

That really was enough. Or too much.

At the Road House Inn, he had a drink, several drinks, that evening with Ms. Baldwin, at the end of which he became maudlin and she, more sympathetic.

They sat at the bar, both smoking, both leaning forward, practically (after a fair while) propped on their arms. He'd said he wanted to talk about Vance, but it began to look as though he really couldn't, as though it hurt him to do so. "Childhood, childhood," he said finally. "It's all about childhood. You ever thought about the lives of the great and good? You ever notice how brief they are about childhood?"

She was coy, too. "I'd like to know about your childhood."

"With vile people like those two, childhood is big."

He thought briefly of taking Pam Baldwin back to the Tam O'Shanter Motel, especially as her hair began to undo and she leaned his way. But then he was overtaken by Vance's childhood, which he'd been putting together piece by piece.

Childhood, he'd been thinking, was the territory of the Little Malices. Of the tiny, subtle pains that are inflicted by all-powerful grown-ups. And though he often thought it was a sick compulsion—born of his own terrors, violent after the death of his own son, Luca—Henning felt he had to dig in there, and he had.

It turned out it wasn't the conventional orphanage and foster-home story, though there were a half-dozen of each he'd turned up in various Welfare archives. That wasn't what had done Vance in. The nuns, who came at the end, when all other remedies had been tried. A place called Saint Joseph's.

The nuns knew they had evil in their midst. The two wings of the building, boys and girls (with the nuns in the middle and a gilded Saint Joseph on top) housed unhappy children, and bad children, and sick children—these could be cared for in God's mercy.

Then there were a very few (as the Mother Superior's letters to her provincial superior revealed) who were simply evil. Was it not their job to extirpate evil?

Item. Sister Angelica, doing her evening lights-out rounds, found Vance standing on his bed and surrounded by younger boys. With his "generative organ" in his hand. A live demonstration if you will. No mention of the organ's "giant proportions" that Benji envied.

Mother Superior took him, barefoot and in only his pajama top, to Jesus in the cold chapel. She made him kiss the Savior's feet and beg forgiveness. She stayed to pray with him, and when it was midnight, sent him back to bed.

The next day, in her office, she showed him how people far better than he had died for Jesus, been grilled, dropped in boiling oil, pulled inside out, hung upside down.

He wouldn't learn, Mother Superior wrote. "Of course he is to be pitied, not knowing who his parents are. But others have been saved. If you look at his record, you will see no one has been able to keep this boy for long."

Just six weeks later, "just for fun," she wrote, he tried to set

Sister Joyce on fire with a rag dipped in the kerosene they used to keep the convent parlor warm the days the occasional parent might come to visit. Before that, he had backed her against the classroom wall after the bell had rung and everyone had gone out into the yard, opened up his fly and pulled out that generative organ of his.

The business with the oily rag was more serious. He was very quick and sly. He waited for her just inside the cloister door just before dinner, when all the other boys were in the refectory. When she came gliding by, her habit swishing, he simultaneously flipped up its hem, lit the rag and pushed it between her knees. She screamed for help and managed to suffocate the flame.

Vance laughed at her and said he wanted to see if a virgin looked any different from just a plain girl. Then he walked out and joined the others in the refectory.

Jesus had still not forgiven him. Vance thought he owed Him a sacrifice. Thus getting washed in the blood of the Lamb.

Maybe—after, he couldn't remember—he told Pam about Herschel, a young man who'd been in group therapy with him after Luca's death.

Unlike Henning, whose background—at least until his father's suicide—was just the opposite of Herschel's, Herschel had spent his entire youth with gangs. Drinking, thieving, whoring, beating up on others, snorting, selling dope. All Jews. As if you'd brought the low life of Odessa to Savannah.

They'd become friends. When they both came out, Herschel showed Henning a page cut out of his high school yearbook: eighteen kids in three rows, about half of whom had white x's on the front of their gowns. Henning asked him what the x's were for, and Herschel said they represented his classmates doing life.

Doing bad things, Herschel explained, was like leprosy. A leper loses sensation in his hand, his nose, his ear; a gang rat loses sensation in his soul, nothing has any meaning for him. It had made Henning think how little one life is like another. He wasn't in that place because his life had been anything like Herschel's.

If Henning did let out that much to Pam Baldwin, after he'd gone to have a slash and washed his face, he soon realized how inappropriate it was to say such things to her. He'd been in her squeaky-clean, ultra-modern office. In fact, he'd sat in her reception area with his hat on his knees, and been, back then, not much more than a mite in the eye of the law. He remembered, looking around Pam's office (when he got in,) how everything in it represented standard, middle America: regular desk and lamp, routine diplomas on the wall, absolutely anyone's carpet.

And facing him (it must have been his first visit) sat, or presided, Ms. Baldwin, a regular thirty-something Texas girl, standard panty-hose, routine worked-over teeth, chest size B-minus, voice whiney, Texas polysyllabic.

What she really liked, she seemed to be saying, was "marinated la-yemb."

"What's that?" he asked, returning to the living. She seeming not to have noted his absence at all. "Washed in the blood of the la-yemb," he thought.

It was a hard job getting through to the ambitious Pamela. Among the many reasons for that was her thinking he fancied her, that he hung around because really, deep down (as they say in that part of the world) he wanted her.

"I said it was one of the things I cook, la-yemb."

Did he? The way women had become in just twenty years, loud-mouthed and cocky, street-smart and emotionally dead, Henning didn't think so. When not falling apart as she was now, she undoubtedly *was* cute (in a big way), bouffant in spirit and hair, resilient as Texans can be.

"Oh, lamb," he said. "I was thinking about Vance."

Again he remembered his first visit to her. Back then (and why would he change now?" he'd concluded that Ms. Baldwin suffered from the sort of moral lockjaw being imported from the two coasts. Just talking about evil wasn't the same thing as knowing it intimately, knowing you might have had in you to be evil too, and for that matter might still. Violence and evil were not things you could keep at a distance. Lennie and Vance had flourished because they had a sense of impunity and an instinct for glorious aggression. What good did it do to apply to them, in a fit of crossness, the higher laws of what was correct behavior? Dear God! Those two were well beyond that. If you abolish the soul in favor of the law, you must expect shame to suffer and only legislation to profit.

She ordered another round. But first she tried to sit up straight on her barstool, reached back with an interesting Bunny-Dip and tried to do something with her hair—which that first time had been so immaculate.

When the drinks came, she said, "Look, I really don't want to know any of this. What's the point? It's revolting. You've obviously got a thing about two deviants who ought to be dead but aren't, and you and I have different reactions. Or rather you don't have any reaction. At least to what I say." At that point she blinked, came into focus, and said, "Vance? I'm trying to put a move on you and you want to talk about Va-yence?"

Remarkable was how her lipstick glistened and her hair waved, how her teeth shone, and her tongue, and her red-ending fingers.

Saevit ira, as Virgil put it: anger let loose. But not unbridled.

"You haven't been listening," Henning said. "I have indeed been thinking about you. I remembered your telling me you had to take a shower…"

"I think you're a dirty old man."

"…after you told the jury the *details* of what was going on."

When Vance let Benji out of the closet, he put a bowl down on the floor and told him to eat his cereal out of that.

"I did," Pam affirmed.

"Did what"

"Did take a shower."

"I think I'm going to take you home."

"Your place or my place," she grinned. "Promise you won't talk about those people?"

"I'm taking you back to your place because I don't think you'd make it back by yourself."

"That's what you say."

No, it was what Henning meant. The three weeks of prep Vance had talked about had ended in October. Everything had ended in October. With the Monday Benji didn't turn up at school or at home.

Chapter thirteen

Mary Kay didn't ask Craig's permission, or whether he wanted the car; she didn't say whether she'd be seeing to their dinner, or he should fend for himself. It was around nine at night, Craig had taken twice as many pain-pills as he needed, and she was worried. She just got into the red pick-up and drove to Hair Today to ask if Benji were there.

He and Lennie had just finished shutting up the salon and it was Vance who walked through the shop to answer the bell. He smiled at Mary Kay and said he hadn't seen Benji since he left the night before. "We figured he was with you ma'am," he said.

This wasn't so. Benji was sleeping off the pills, being tied up and humiliated right over her head. Vance had had to do the cleaning up in the salon, and Lennie was upstairs. Both of them had said they weren't really hungry.

Mary Kay had on her little-girl smile that went with her short skirt and the little white blouse with a brooch pinned at her collar. She said, "I wonder where he might be."

"Might be with that Ron."

"Oh? I don't think so, Vance. You know he broke Craig's arm. I thought he was going to take the truck and drive off in it. Instead, as I was helping Craig into the house and I asked him to leave the truck so I could take Craig to the hospital, he said he'd be all right. He was leaving town, he said. The only thing he wanted was say goodbye to you and Benji, and how sorry he was."

"He never did that. Come by here."

"Then I guess he must be on his way home. I think he said he lived in California."

"He'll be somewhere, ma'am, that's for sure."

"You haven't seen my Benji? Anywhere at all?"

"He didn't show up for work. I thought maybe he was sick or something."

"He didn't go to school, either. He's never missed school."

"Maybe he did see Ron, though I told him not to."

It could have been, Henning thought, that Benji had woken up from one of his drug-induced "sleeps" or just wanted to go to the bathroom. (One of the items on Lennie's list—it was Number 11 and came after a long list of supplies Vance was to buy, but not in Sapphire—was "tape the windows with black garbage liners like a darkroom. Do the same to the door and take out the light-bulb in the hall upstairs.") That would account for Lennie just then putting on *Die Fledermaus* real loud.

Down below, Mary Kay started singing along with it. "Isn't that just beautiful music? Lennie loves music, doesn't he?" She waltzed a bit with herself and that made her skirt bounce around her slim hips. It was the look that drove Craig crazy.

"What should I do?" she asked. "You think I should tell the police?"

"Not yet, I wouldn't. I mean, he could be sitting back home waiting for you."

"I've only been gone a half-hour."

"I tell you what. You go on home. Lennie and I are going to go get us something to eat and we'll have a look-around."

"But it's dark. It's his bedtime. I thought he might be sleeping here. You know, got the day wrong or something. Where does he sleep when he stays over?"

"Out back, on the back porch."

"Can I see?"

"Sure."

Vance was taking her out back when the sound of the music was amplified, meaning Lennie's door had opened, and Lennie came down. "I saw you dancing down here, Mrs. Rapp, My mother used to dance the way you do."

"Oh my, Mr. Crace! You surely do know how to make a lady feel good. I just dropped by to see if my Benji wasn't here."

Lennie looked at Vance. "Didn't he say something yesterday about choir? That it was starting up again?" Vance, not quick enough, mumbled something unintelligible. "Sure, because his voice was breaking, he had to sing something for Mr. Moyes."

"Oh thank you so much," Mary Kay said, as Vance opened the back door for her.

"Now you dance all the way to that fine truck of yours, Mrs. Rapp!" Lennie said. One-TWO-three, one-TWO-three."

But Lennie's mood soon changed. Where were Vance's brains? If Mrs. Rapp thought Ron was coming by here, it was that she had a pretty good idea he would. And what if somebody asked her what happened to Ron after he broke Craig's arm?

Vance said, "Aw shit, Ron ain't going to talk to no one."

"Even dead people talk. And what did you put in the Kid's feed?"

"Just Tender Loving Care."

"It's no joke."

"I gave him what you said exactly. A little high, a lot of low, Fentanil, Norflex. His eyeballs must be rolling."

"You gave him exactly as many as I told you? He's moving around a lot in there. He give you any problems when you fed him?"

"He was eager."

"I'll bet."

"You wouldn't know. That's between us."

"Send him home anyway. Untie him and send him home. Give him a nice kiss, tell him he's been a good boy, tell him his Ma's worried and tell him we'll see him again on Friday."

Vance didn't say what he thought—What Benji might say to his mother—because just as he was about to do so he realized Lennie was right. Benji would be back. By now this was the only place he existed, the only place where he had a friend who could both hurt him and humiliate him and love him and comfort him.

Henning had asked Lennie why, if he thought Vance was unreliable, if he was a risk, didn't he call the whole thing off?

Lennie said: "You're like the rest of them. You think I planned the whole thing. *That* way? You're nuts. What I 'planned' and what happened are two different things."

Henning had dropped into the VFW with Sheriff Overmayer on several Friday nights, the Friday night in particular, the first one Craig felt well enough to go out. And get good and drunk. As Craig announced as he came through the door.

You didn't go just because it was there, the drinks were cheap, and the company was the kind you cared to get drunk with. For the Nam people in Sapphire, and a few who'd done Korea and even World War Two, going there was something they *had* to do. And they got drunk because then they could go over stories no one else was interested in hearing. Because drinking cut away the wall built between those who'd been there, like himself, and those who hadn't: for instance Mary Kay's two "long-gone and worthless" (her Daddy's words) brothers who'd been down in Austin at U.T. throughout.

As far as Craig was concerned, Nam was the only thing that mattered. He'd been one sort of man before he was drafted and another when he came back. It was the same story with many others. As he put it, it was a rare month he or one of the others didn't hear that so-and-so had topped himself, gone off the road, been whacked into one of the VA hospitals.

The main reason he went, however, was that he felt compelled to talk about it, because if he didn't, no one would. Talking about it reminded him Nam had been real. The silence of everyone else made it seem Nam had never happened. But his body remembered its pain, and the drink helped with that.

Friday nights you could bring guests, but not women. They had Ladies Nights for women and they watched their language.

Craig wished they couldn't bring in people who hadn't done his war, but he was outvoted. As long as they'd been in the Service, and Lennie—though Craig despised him—had been, they were welcome. It helped keep the Post going and they needed to reach out to the young people, on account of the Nam people were slipping over fifty and then some. "Given the choice," he said, "I'd have drawn the line at Vance. I can't explain how he ever got to be a regular. Some guys thought he was a card. I didn't."

Sheriff Overmayer was a regular. Overmayer was a short, com-pact man with steel-rimmed glasses, thinning, sandy hair, and legs so bowed it looked like he'd been born with a horse between his legs.

"You understand," Craig went on, Henning buying, Overmayer listening sympathetically, "I didn't really pay much heed to those two. I remember that night because it was the first time I really studied them. The Kid hadn't come home the Monday before and I'd got into a slanging match with Mary Kay 'bout that. I guess I was scared for the boy. Mary Kay was scared, too. But it was Benji who scared her; she couldn't figure him out. And she sure as hell didn't understand Lennie and Vance. I couldn't stand Vance, but he didn't really bother me: I figured him for just a punk who tagged along with Lennie. But you get to thinking about people like Lennie who're loners, who stand apart at the bar just looking at people, not drinking, who hardly ever say a thing, play ball with you, but not really *with* you—people like that are kind of scary. Still, all I knew about him then was that if you wanted weed or something else, he was your man."

The night Benji came back to Hair Today—oh yes, he'd come back all right, and lay passed out and sprawled across Vance's bed—Sheriff Overmayer walked in around ten at night. The place was already jumping.

First he had a couple of shots of bourbon, straight, then he started asking around: anyone there know what had happened to the big biker called Ron, "The guy who was right here with us some weeks back?"

At the time the sheriff started asking questions, Vance was up on a table with a shiny silky dress on, stockings and ruffled garters up above his knees.

This was another of his numbers. He was the Wild West's whore with the heart of gold. He did one of his imitations every time he was there. Walking right through town round nine dressed up and without a care in the world. Then, by popular demand he'd get down to his business, and even Craig had to admit he could be funny as all get-out.

That night, he said, he'd been standing by the pianist who was playing for the gussied-up Vance. The pianist was the Volunteer Fire Chief, a half-Indian. He could play a bunch of honky-tonk tunes from when they'd been in Saigon on leave. "Most everyone was singing—not Lennie of course, he was making the rounds selling raffle tickets for the High School Band, frigging hypocrite—and Vance was kicking his pretty legs up (O my DARling!) high one side and (O my DARling!) high the other."

When the Sheriff asked him about Ron, he said sure he remembered him, "said he was from some Post in California. No one asked for ID or anything like that."

Of course everybody knew about the fight Craig had had with Ron and how Ron had broken his arm so Craig was off work for a couple of weeks. But the Sheriff was cool about that and didn't ask Craig anything else. Instead, he sat down at the table Vance was dancing on, and asked again.

Then Lennie strolled over and said to Vance, "Get off the goddam table, Vance. The Sheriff here's got a question."

Craig said Vance blushed like a girl. "Frigging clown! He climbs down and sashays round the table, sits down next to the Sheriff, straightens out his dress, and rests his head on Overmayer's shoulder. No common sense at all. He says to the Sheriff, 'Won't you buy me a drink, honey?' Now Lennie wants to know why the Sheriff's asking."

The Sheriff said he was asking on account of some off-road dune-buggy maniac found a body. A guy all rigged out in leather and studs and boots, patches and stuff. Overmayer said: "It gave him such a shock he crashed into a boulder."

"He was no biker," said Lennie. "Just a big turd."

"Maybe so, but he's dead and his hands were taped behind him and had tape round his eyes and mouth. I don't reckon he did that to himself or just walked off the highway where there's nothing around for miles. I know you and Craig saw him that night, you all must have seen him. Anyone seen him since?"

"Big fat queer," the fire chief said from his piano. "I remember him. You took him home Craig. Or he took you home's more likely."

That got a laugh.

But nobody said they'd seen Captain Ron since that night.

The Sheriff said he didn't figure they had. "Down where they found this guy, they said he'd been brained with a rock. "Had a piece of paper all scrunched up in the pocket of his jacket with the name of Mary Kay's boy Benji on it and her address at the farm, which is why they called me up in case we'd seen him around. I said I'd seen him, but not since a month ago. Benji works at your shop doesn't he?"

"Weekends," Vance said, still standing around but looking silly in his dress. "Benji ran into him in town. Told me about it. His name's Ron, calls himself a captain. Boy at the Dairy Queen ought to remember him, that's where he was. Haven't seen him myself. Except here of course. They sure it's him? People down there?"

"He have a slit up the back of his jacket when he was here?"

"A slit?"

"About that slit, Craig said to Henning. "I'd have seen that, so would Mary Kay. I don't remember no slit. I said that to the Sheriff."

"Not really a slit," the sheriff said. "A piece about two inches wide going right up to his collar in back. Cut real neat. Maybe with scissors or a razor blade."

"I didn't see a slit," said Lennie.

"Now hold on," said the sheriff. "All that means is someone cut that out of his jacket after he left here. You tell me why."

A piece of leather from which Vance, as Lennie well knew, had fashioned a collar with metal studs which he tied round Benji's neck, saying, "So's you know whose dog you are." A collar which the principal had confiscated from Benji and given back at the end of the school day only because Benji said he wouldn't wear it to school any more, it had great sentimental value, being the only thing he had from his Dad.

Chapter fourteen

The closer you got to the end, Henning thought, the harder it got. It seemed that starting with death and working backwards, the tissue of life thickened and some idea of what this threesome "really" was like emerged. But also there was a death at the end, and that was always painful to face. No one wanted to look at the event itself, the necessary, inevitable act. By then, like the always-efficient Nava County prosecutor, Henning had found out things about Lennie he'd rather not have known, and knew there were still things he didn't know he might like even less.

The first image that had come to him about Lennie—long before he decided to go out to Sapphire—was that of a spider: a genial contemporary spider with blue denim legs a bit shorter than the average spider's, big frank eyes ("*Me*? Hurt you?"), short careful fur. An *interesting* spider. A spider whose web, if one were not a fly or his prey, one could study with pleasure, the spokes of its wheel, the radials that bind it, or with the horror one feels for unseen things in the night. The image had stuck with him.

The big thing Lennie had in common with a spider was his sheer, awful loneliness. Because like a spider, Lennie needed, just to live, that his prey come to him.

It so happened Sapphire's one-day-a-week library had a book about spiders, and Mrs. Spenser pulled it out for him. He read that:

Among the threads, which entangle the wings and legs of inter-cepted prey, the spiders are perfectly at home and can pounce on the struggling victim at once if it be small and harmless or keep at a respect-ful distance, checking all attempts at escape, if it is poisonous or strong. If in the latter case the spider is afraid to come to close quarters, various devices for securing it are resorted to… [Some] eject onto the insect… drops of liquid adhesive silk… [Others] steadying it… sweep additional strands of silk over it… [Still others] attaching a long thread to a point hard by, run round and round the victim in circles, gradually winding it up beyond all hope of breaking loose.

He read the passage out loud to Mrs. Spenser, because it had given him pleasure. That was Nature all right, he told her. Nature knows all about the food chain, reproduction and the elementary cruelty necessary for survival. The spider, hidden in its own web, full of receptors and alarms, sensitive to the most minute change in the tension of a strand hides, is condemned to eternal waiting for the frivolous, excited insect on which it will feed.

Neither the spider nor Lennie cared what (or who) that prey was.

That night he wrote a letter to his former wife Ludi, Luca's mother. As he had always been with her, even when she had divorced him, he was absolutely straight. That is, about the conditions of the real world as he saw them. And thinking about Luca and Benji both, who came to unhappy ends, and also about people who behaved like Lennie and Vance, he wrote: "You know, the struggle for existence used to be about moral choices. You could be bad and you could be good. But I've come to realize that there are situations in which these choices have no meaning it all. One does what one has to do just to be able to go on living."

What brought that to mind was one of his last conversations with Lennie, working his way up to the crime itself, in which he'd asked Lennie if he wasn't at least aware of the pain he might be inflicting on the boy.

Lennie said no. What boy? It could have been anyone. There was nothing personal about it. There was no Benji who was Mary Kay's son, who went to the local Middle School, who looked and dressed in a particular way. In fact, the question had seemed to exasperate him. Was Vance someone? No. Anyone. He said, "I don't ask myself questions like that."

In fact, Henning realized, Lennie had never asked himself questions of any kind.

When his mother called him in from the garden—"Leonard! I know you're out there!"—he was otherwise absorbed. He heard all right, because hearing her call increased the pleasure he felt in observation. Something was happening. To him and in front of him. Any garden was full of sanitary, necessary deaths, and these gave Lennie a foretaste of his whole life. The attraction of a garden lay in the anonymity of its flora and fauna, its flowers and wee beasties. Why should he care that an apple rotted and ants carried off carrion?

"You tell me," he said, "What's the big fuss about human beings? They're somehow different?"

He didn't hear his mother as a mother. She was a distraction. She had nothing to do with the web in which destruction took place; whereas others buzzed and flew in.

First time he saw Hope, he sensed her end: her long legs caught in the wheel of her bike sliding under the dark waters. Same with the Number One Boy's head held tightly in Hal's hands, the prisoners in a web of iron bars and burning, Benji bound in meticulous tape.

When he met them or saw them, there was a quivering of expectation, an appreciable excitement.

On the fatal night, Lennie had twenty-seven dollars collected from the sale of raffle tickets in his back pocket and he made the little lying bastard Vance walk ahead of him back up Houston Street from the VFW Post, stopping him at the bank where he carefully deposited the money in the deposit window. As always, he read all the instructions and double-checked that his slip tallied.

He was in that particular state that he'd learned to tune in to. It was a state in which time slowed down and his powers of observation were greatly magnified. The bench by the bus-stop, for instance, which advertised local businesses, took on an almost scriptural quality, as though its words had been carved in stone and handed down by Moses; on a candy wrapper that drifted by in the barely perceptible after-midnight breeze, he could make out with ease its many ingredients.

When he started up again toward the Salon, with Vance the same precise distance ahead of him, there was a displaced seam on the seat of Vance's jeans. He noted the seam because disorder of any kind upset him. He could count the scuffmarks on the heels of Vance's baskets.

He said to Vance, "Slow down, we're in no hurry."

This always happened: in the garden back home, on the embankment in Davenport, Iowa, on Guam, seeing Donnellan at the Burger King or Vance standing by him at the bar. Time expanded. As good hitters can count the stitches on a baseball, seconds expanded into minutes and minutes into hours. Time had big black holes in which there was a special kind of peace and an extreme light.

Like the minutes that precede an epileptic fit, Henning noted.

Who had also noted that on the inventory of books and papers taken from Lennie's room facing the street above the salon were both *Crime and Punishment* and *The Idiot*. But according to all his medical reports, Lennie was in perfect health. Unless one wants to count literature as a form of sickness.

Lennie had said: "You must know what it's like. If you know something's going to happen, you also know all the steps that lead up to it. The last second before an accident, the car coming straight at you, you're paralyzed. But suppose you're in the other car and you *want* to drive straight at it, every inch between you and it is like a mile long. Nothing distracts you."

Lennie seemed to be saying that when you saw things that clearly, what you were facing was revelation. It wasn't like seeing something again and vaguely feeling you've seen it before, like déjà vu. No; he had a clear insight into something that was happening: "even if you regret it, or wish it wouldn't."

Henning said: unless your intention is subverted by some fundamental miscalculation. Surely Vance was a wrong step?

"There are no wrong steps," said Lennie angrily.

Then it's a "fate", is it?

"When I was a kid, they sent me out on a snipe hunt. I was bound to get lost, find my way back late, open the door, and walk in on Hal getting blown. I felt sorry for him, that he needed that, but I wasn't going to stop it happening… or Hope. When I first met her, I knew."

As if the steps in his life were written down somewhere. Its text told him Vance in his femme get-up would dance on the table, the sheriff would ask about Ron's body, his skull crushed with a rock, the dune-buggy rider would crash into a boulder, he himself would walk back with Vance and deposit the raffle money—No need to hurry!

And Vance did slow down as Lennie ordered, clutching his Wild West dress, scarlet, and garters, pink-and-silver and ruched, over his arm: in memory of the only girl from an 1860s saloon with a Rolex on her wrist.

They both loitered. Looked in shop windows, one or two still lit at that hour, that contained nothing they didn't know by heart. Passed the gas station, Texaco, that would stay open all night: in whose convenience store Vance was going to go out and buy them sandwiches in the early hours.

The night was cool and very dry.

Lennie unlocked the front door to the Salon, its chairs neatly covered in the sheets they wrapped round the ladies, and snapped on the lights to check the appointment book. "Looks like a busy day tomorrow," he said. "Ten to one, solid."

Vance made as if to walk through the salon and into the kitchen, which was behind. He knew Lennie was sore about the sheriff and Ron's body being found. When something happened that wasn't really his fault (How could he know that some rich kid would take his dune buggy out just there?), or at least something he hadn't meant to do, his first urge was always to explain. The trouble was, no one ever listened to him. Certainly not Lennie, who was in one of his ice-cold moods.

Vance could form the words in his head, he couldn't get them out. So he had to play them out silently in his head.

The way it happened was that Ron's hands had been tied when he got out of the car, he was scared, he was shaking, and he tripped, hit his head on a rock.

That was all right. Stupid bastard that he was, he deserved to trip and bang his head. The only important thing was that Ron should get lost and never come back. Because without Ron there was nothing that had happened, or would happen, that the sheriff could connect them to.

Of course all he got out was, "I'll go up and see how the Kid is."

Lennie said, "No hurry."

Vance sat down in one of the chairs and swung around in it, stockings fallen down around his ankles, where they formed something like cattle-ponds; tan water in tan land.

"After this you've got to go," Lennie said. "One last big one and you're out of here. I think you can understand that."

"And you?" Vance asked, clinging to the dress on his lap. What he wanted most at that moment was that Lennie should touch him. Any form of human contact. Vance meant his gestures to be seductive. He crossed his arms and laid his hands on his shoulders, as little girls do to make their tits seem bigger. Then he reached forward and picked up a comb and readjusted his parting, the fine blond hair that he built up in front, the back that had a touch of curl.

As Lennie didn't answer, he thought idly of their early days, the YMCA in Saint Louis, and the way he'd rejoiced at the pair they were! And then, in some other place (it seemed) Lennie talking about threesomes, good threesomes and bad threesomes.

Just minutes ago, Lennie was still talking to him, telling him what to do. Now he was being told to get out.

Lennie and Benji were the only family he'd ever had.

Still cold, Lennie said: "Don't you worry about me. You worry about yourself. When you're done down here, you go get the kid ready."

Done down here? What was there to do? He said: "What you want of me, Lennie?"

Lennie was over at the lock-box under the cash register, from which he took out ten hundreds, folding them neatly and laying them out under the mirror in front of Vance's chair. In his other hand he had a little clutch of pills, which he set down alongside the bills.

"You've got to perform," he said. "Take these. It's going to be a long night for you and the bus leaves oh-six-five-oh so the money's to get you where you want to go, and the little blue-and-yellow ones, they're to bring you down so you don't embarrass yourself in front of the good Trailways people."

"And Benji?"

"You mean for now? Or after? After he goes home. After you go one way and I go another. The bank will sell the place and I'll send you a share. But now—well you know how it is with the delights of this world, you can't take 'em with you. All those religious things circulating in your head, that's good. You can be thinking of that while you get to work. Like what they're going to be saying when they put what's left of Ron in the ground. Naked you come into the world and all that, dust to dust. For right now, Jesus is just waiting to see how you *perform*. So you swallow that lot. Trust me. Then you get all the shit laid out up in your room like it says on the list. If the kid's asleep, wake him up; if he's got his pants on, take 'em off. Jesus only knows what you're going to do without me."

On Vance's arrest report, under "distinguishing marks," it says: "tattoo below navel, *Ecce Agnus Dei*." Behold the Lamb of God.

Henning thought something didn't quite fit. Lennie drives the Kid back to Mary Kay's, nice knowing you, and the Kid keeps his mouth shut?

In court, Vance's lawyer, a local attorney, Sam Hoxey, got his client to burst into tears and say he thought Lennie would kill him if he didn't do what he ordered. Was that why he didn't take the pills Lennie gave him until he was upstairs, the scene was being staged, and Lennie took up his usual position in the door of Vance's room and held out a glass of water, watching him until he'd swallowed the pills?

Chapter fifteen

Pam Baldwin had invited him to dinner, "at *my* house," for her "marinated la-yemb"—"I owe you at least a dinner," was the graciously nasal way she put it. On Henning's mind were the lawyers: Lennie's, Jon Eastling, and Vance's, Sam Hoxey. What was on Ms. Baldwin's mind?

Hoxey had had the harder time of it, and making Lennie out to be the arch-demon reflected badly on his own client. The town was full of people who saw and knew just how *queer* Vance was (in any sense of the word a jury might understand), and as many people, like Mary Kay, or Homer the banker, or his mates on the softball team, were available to say in court that what happened was awful but not quite believable about a guy who in many ways was likeable and respectable. If he weren't, why would Mary Kay have entrusted her precious little Benji to Lennie?

With what he had to work with—a deviant client and a hostile town—Henning thought Hoxey had done a decent job. He had put forward a case that fitted the facts as Henning saw them, that Lennie had forced Vance, a younger man, unstable and not very bright, to act, and that Benji had been complicit from the start.

His feelings about Eastling were mixed. Henning had talked to him once or twice, but without result. He didn't much like it that his fees had been paid out of a trust-fund set up for him by his grandmother when Lennie was born and not by his parents, nor did he think Eastling had done much of a job for Lennie. He had based his whole defense on two foundations: Lennie's abnormal life, traumas under which he'd finally broken, and a *denial* that Lennie had ever so much as *touched* Benji or any other minor.

And then there was Pam. He thought she'd had an easy time of it. The two men were bound together. Like husband and wife, they'd pleaded guilty together, and were, in the Prosecution's eyes, equally guilty. It was all down there on paper. Lennie had written out his instructions—the jurors could read them in their horrid detail—and Vance had carried them out to the letter.

Luckily Nava wasn't a dry country, and Henning found two bottles of a pretty good Burgundy in a liquor store, got directions to Pam's house, drove out there and up there, and climbed, bottles clanking, up to her ranch-house pad.

Once ensconced—dinner bubbled in the background and a spectacularly large and spicy Bloody Mary nestled in Henning's hand—a few desultory remarks, to the effect that he'd been thinking about the trial, quickly revealed that Ms. Baldwin, Nieman Marcus pants-suit and all, was turned on by lawyer-talk. Anyway, turned on.

Psychology was not her thing, nor certainly was history or, for that matter were literature or the arts. They talked law. How she'd made her way up, why she'd chosen prosecution over private practice (politics), and what was wrong with criminal lawyers in general and Sam Hoxey in particular. She wiped the floor with Hoxey—"another bleeding liberal." She said she found people bleeding in public not a nice sight. Further, he had no sense of the public interest. About Eastling, she was circumspect. But Eastling did know about the public interest, because he had helped get the trial over and done with, fast.

When they had dinner—they got through Henning's two bottles of Burgundy and then a Sauterne she kept in a closet behind a dozen severe power-suits and brought in with a Baked Alaska—she retired for some time to the bathroom while Henning busied himself with blowing on Texan embers, mesquite and something, in her fireplace.

She came back in, barefoot and silent, and put her jeweled hands over his eyes. When she let go and he turned round, he found her reclining on the rich, red carpet, naked. So silent for a big girl, she was offering him her pubis, that furry animal that clung to her lower belly. It was of pure spun gold. Eminent and heterosexual—a relief.

On the other hand, as Henning knew, this sort of thing did not happen very often

in real life. Nor had sex crossed his mind recently. So what sort of ploy was this?

Modern girls like Pam generally thrived on adversarial terrain, not submission. Yet there was no doubt about it: just then she was supine.

First he thought she might be offering him a challenge: "Come and get it!" And despite the cordial talk and the wine, Henning was pretty sure she hadn't undergone a change of feeling about him. He was what he was. He knew himself to be neither wild nor exotic. Nor even sexy. She had to know that.

His second, unworthy, thought was that she wanted him to try and fail. She'd be eloquent with pants and fast and loose with her mouth, then she'd say, "Better luck next time" or "Better luck next girl." There was no perception more likely than that one to drive a man his age to the higher moral ground. Not here, not now, not on your terms, what do you want?

Finally, seeing as her eyes were closed, her lips moist, her arms welcoming, he decided that she just wanted to get laid and was bored with the locals.

The sex was discreet. She performed with the directness and inconsequentiality modern American girls have learned of late, a sort of cheery concentration in which wetness was all, well-trained muscles were sent splendidly into play, and the whole thing was so light-hearted and transitory that no feeling of any sort could so much as displace a hair.

The truth was that Pam's mind was mired in a Sargasso Sea of weed, wine and addresses to the only juror present, himself.

During and after she could and did talk to the top of his head or his navel. What transpired was, to her credit, that she was satisfyingly excited by the sheer mystery Henning offered. What was he really doing in Sapphire? What brought a man of his breeding and education to kow-tow to foul strays (she actually said "sprays") like Vance and Lennie?

"I really came out here to seduce you," he said. "I was told that prosecuting attorneys out in the Wild West invariably turn up, one day or another, on a carpet in front of an open fire."

That earned him ten minutes of silent busyness, her hands, which were strong and well cared-for, did their business as though she were searching for a penny in the bottom of a vast purse.

In the process he did learn quite a bit about the law, or at least how it was practiced up here in the Panhandle. For instance, the moves she'd had to make to get assigned to the case.

After another visit, yawning, to the bathroom and now arrayed in a full-length robe of Chinese flowered silk, she sat down next to him on the carpet and said, "Thank you. That was very nice."

Thus satisfied, she said she would now try to answer some of his questions, since otherwise he would go on making a pest of himself instead of acting like the perfectly nice human being he obviously was.

"Eastling?"

"Eastling didn't want the job. I wouldn't want you to think he didn't do the best he could, but like any normal person would, he found his client a sick psychopath. Someone best put away."

"Queer never came up in court."

"They pleaded guilty."

"The press didn't talk about queer either."

"What a sheltered life you must lead," she said, stroking

Henning's cheek. "No one had to say anything. The jury had only to look at them. Out here, queer is funny, it's something you make fun of."

"And they didn't seduce Benji?"

End of sex and friendliness. Untangling her legs and rising up to her full five-ten-and-a-half, she said: "They didn't effing seduce the boy. They raped him. There's a difference."

Chapter sixteen

Eastling hadn't wanted the case? Why not? Henning checked the transcript of the trial and something else popped up at him: Eastling's insistence, throughout the trial (mercifully brief), that he represented the family, the way he always referred to Lennie as "the Defendant" rather than "my client."

Henning figured going up North to Washington State was just about the last thing he had to do.

Eastling wasn't at all what Henning had expected. He was cherubic. He was round, curly, dark, sixtyish, and on the short side; also edgy, saturnine, deliberate. His office was wood-paneled and dusky, with a Tiffany lamp (authentic) on his desk. After two curt refusals, he finally received Henning—who sensed right away that Eastling saw him as a kite he could fly, one whose strings he held.

Like many of the lawyers Henning had met in the course of business, Eastling was a specialist in evasion. He also had annoying tic which made him laugh (*"her-her"*) at inappropriate places, viz: "You were out here once before, at least down in San Jose, weren't you, Professor, *her-her*? So Frank told me. He wasn't pleased. He called me up to make sure you didn't repeat the visit." It was a peculiar laugh, dry like old spice left in the bottom of a jar.

"Oh? He sounded friendly enough."

"You probably noticed Frank doesn't talk much, save to himself. Not for years. What you'd call a taciturn man. Doesn't like to be disturbed."

"I didn't notice that. Nervous maybe."

"Be that as it may, just what might your purpose be in coming all this way?"

"I'd like to find Lennie's folks—He told me his family had moved back up here, didn't like California– and I was hoping you might be able to fill in a few things about Lennie's past."

"Tell you that, did he? Leonard didn't talk much either. When he was a boy."

"He does now. Is his father here?"

"He might be," Eastling said doubtfully. "Last time he said that if you bothered him again I was to get an injunction against you."

Henning remained polite. "Could you tell me why?"

"Perhaps I could."

"Well? If your client talks to me, why wouldn't you?"

Eastling's tone changed. He tugged at his waistcoat, adjusted his bow tie; his voice turned inflexible. "Leonard is not *my* client. We could begin there. I was retained by his family. And there are lots of reasons why I would hesitate to talk to you. Professionally, that is. The first is that you have no standing. Less now than you might have had two years ago during the trial. Then you might have been passed off as an inquiring reporter, though they too were discouraged. The fact is, you don't belong in this case; yet you're insistent, and no one knows why. You say Leonard talks to you, but he might have reasons for so doing. He might want to know what you've found out. Because frankly, Leonard, as I've said, *her-her*, is not the talkative sort. There is also a distinct possibility that he might wish to mislead you; and you, not knowing the facts of the case, or much about Leonard's past, could easily fall into error."

"I could ask you, whose side are you on?"

"Whose side of what, Mr. Forsell? I was under the impression that Texas v. Crace had been adjudicated, and sentence passed."

"I only ask because on reading the transcript…"

"You thought Leonard had been short-changed? But as I've explained, I represent the family, and my duty is to the family. To the extent that I was instructed to do so, I think I was reasonably successful for Leonard. Given, if you take my meaning, feelings in a little Texas town. There are a lot of things a non-lawyer might not understand about legal obligations. I did what I could to present to the jury the fact that even though Leonard might know right from wrong—the classic *mens rea*, the ability to make up his mind, to know what he's doing, and therefore be responsible for it—he was not what anyone would call 'normal'. Some minds are not 'mad' but seriously distorted. Seriously and permanently. There was also much I couldn't say because of the fashion in which I had been instructed, by his trust, of which I'm one of the executors, and by Frank. I have to say that, professionally, I don't think I can be of any help to you."

It was the second time that he used the word "professionally". It was worth a try, so I asked him if there were any other way in which he might be able to help.

"That," he replied, "would depend on you and on what your real interest is in this case."

"What do you mean?"

"Well, I obviously can't stop you asking questions. I can only deter you from infringing on poor Frank's privacy. What you find out on your own is your business."

"Why is he 'poor Frank'?"

"Because of Leonard. Because of Millie. Because he's walked the streets of this little town delivering the mail for thirty years and everyone knows him, so he feels ashamed. Because he's half Swedish, because he's gloomy, because he drinks, because he doesn't *understand*. What more do you want to know? Frank is a simple, hard-working man caught up in matters that are really beyond his ken. He doesn't understand them, he never will. He's done everything he could with the life he was given, but to no avail. There are certain things you cannot rid yourself of, and even if I were to let you speak to him, I assure you would get nothing from him."

"His mother, then. He seems to be close to her. He writes her every week, he told me."

Eastling gave Henning a sad, and triumphant, little smile. "Millicent, his mother, poor soul, has been dead these thirty years now, Professor. I don't think she can help you."

After a week's work up there in the territory of Lennie's childhood Henning understood why Lennie's lawyer couldn't help. His responsibility began and ended with Frank Crace and the trust. That week Henning spent interviewing, when they were willing, anyone who knew or had an inkling of the family's history. Every day that went by he was more disturbed by the sheer dimension of Lennie's lies, about those letters to which no reply ever came. The worst sort of conjectures went through his mind, and each time he talked to someone he lived in fear of what he might learn about Millicent's death, about which Eastling had refused to give any details. As he said in a call back to Pam Baldwin, it was like being in hell without a guidebook. A lot of people here were lost souls, literally. They didn't know, they couldn't remember, it was so long ago: as though they all shared in some generalized disgrace that had struck the town.

One exception was Mrs. Pimen, Frank Crace's mother. When he went to see her in her nursing home, she'd obviously been told what he was after. She rose in her wrath, all sixty pounds of her clutching the aluminum rims of her wheelchair wheels, and shouted, "That bitch! She ruined Frank's life and everyone's. I'm glad she's dead before me. She got what was coming to her."

But that was obviously all she could bring herself to say. Hatred had exhausted her and the nurses had to hustle her away to canasta. She was coming up to ninety: was she of sound mind?

But Henning continued to sit there in her room, and when she came back she didn't seem surprised to see Henning sitting there.

"What did Millicent get that she had coming to her?" he asked.

She shook her head vigorously and pressed her lips together with a frail hand.

It wasn't that she wouldn't talk; she couldn't. She'd stored up her energy to say as much as she had.

A nurse came in and said, "You have no right. …You're agitating Mrs. Pimen." He was, and she was right to ask him to leave.

When his Luca died, how had Henning felt about the questions being asked him? Getting to the truth was a terrible burden: borne equally by those who had something to hide and those who had to find out. And who was he to stir things up? Who would think "understanding" was reason enough, when the past could still hurt the living?

Henning went to all the usual places in Frank's hometown, where he and Millie had lived and Lennie had grown up. He saw the lumber mill, the disused station, the schools, full of fresh-faced youths who were still alive and had no sense that they night not be.

He even drove slowly past Frank's house. A house in which nothing seemed to move, or to have moved in many years. There were rhododendrons out front, thick, wet, and pulpy. A flagstone path led up to the front door, which had a screen. Maybe some houses had been built around Lennie's childhood home, because the garden behind didn't look big enough for Lennie to hide in there from his mother. All Henning could see was a patch of lawn and a wood fence at its end, not very well kept up.

He wanted to be inconspicuous, so when he met people by chance, people Frank Crace's age, he would never ask a direct question, nor mention Frank, or Millie, or Lennie. Nobody seemed to have heard of the case in Texas; Lennie was never mentioned. He wasn't a cop; he had no right to push them. Some of them did talk, but to pass the time of day. But only about Frank, whom they thought the world of. He was retired. A lot of people thought he'd gone to California. No one had seen him recently.

One night, in a bar down the block from his motel, Henning said, standing his neighbors a drink, Henning said he'd been on

Guam with a soldier who said he came from here and his father was a mailman. Being perfectly casual.

A mailman? That had to be Frank. Didn't he have a boy who went into the service?

Sure, Lennie, someone said. Haven't thought about him for years. Yeah, I remember. Nice-looking boy. Very polite.

Someone else said, wasn't there some scandal. You know, years ago?

Henning made out that wasn't of any interest to him. He said, "Well, it was just a coincidence, my passing through on business. I mean, I suddenly remembered that Lennie, that was his name all right, had said he came from a little town. There's a lumber mill, right?"

Something about Frank's wife, said the first man.

"Is she still alive?"

No. Frank's been a widower as long as I've been here.

Henning stolidly drank his beer, and heard, or thought he heard, Millie calling her son in from the garden, "Leonard!" If Millie had been dead thirty years, this would have been when Lennie was under ten. "Leonard? I know you're out there!"

If he'd been able to see Frank, he would at least have some idea what Millie looked like. There would have been a wedding photograph or something. Or maybe there wouldn't have been. The days were clear out there in Washington State, the nights were clear. Coming up to winter, the air had a bite. But nothing else was clear.

Having no idea when Millie was supposed to have died, he didn't expect much when he went to the public library and looked through the files of what had once been the local newspaper. And yet, not more than five minutes into turning its fragile pages, he came across what he wanted.

Millicent had died on December 24th, 1968. A Mrs. Sullivan had found the body and called the police. The week after, he read that the funeral service had been "private."

A clear-sighted, clear-minded woman in her early fifties, Maggie Sullivan was alive, she was at home, and she was willing to tell Henning what she knew.

"Miss Millicent," as Mrs. Sullivan called her, came from a prosperous wine-growing family in the eastern part of the state, the other side of the mountains. She was very much a "lady" in her manners, her expectations and her speech. Mrs. Sullivan did not know where she and Frank married, but she'd been with the family since before Leonard was born, and she'd been hired by Millie's mother through an agency.

Her first impression when she took up her "position" was that, despite the fact that Millie looked six months pregnant, the two young people seemed "just married." Not that they behaved "the way turtle-doves are supposed to do." Quite the contrary. "It was as if they hardly knew one another. I was living in at the time, so I'd prepare breakfast for Miss Millicent and Mr. Frank. At the time Mr. Frank wasn't with the mail, he was a pharmacist's assistant. I remember asking Mr. Frank what sort of cereal I should be buying for Miss Millicent's breakfast. He said I ought to be asking her. I thought that a wee bit odd."

There were other signs, too. They didn't seem very affectionate, and Miss Millicent was very much the boss—"I suspected that might be because of the disparity in money, she having more than he—and then, when "little Leonard, a lovely baby," was born, "there wasn't any of the usual fuss with a new baby. Like a stranger he was.

"She had the baby at home, I assisted her with a midwife, and we were both struck by the way she behaved. Not by her 'distraction', which I didn't think much of that at the time, because young mothers are often a bit at sea with a first child, but by the way she viewed birthing as something she had to go through, not crying or shouting or anything, just biting her lip and letting it happen to her. And it wasn't an easy birth, not at all: she was at it from five in the morning until three o'clock in the afternoon. Then when the midwife put the baby to her breast, she said, 'No, I'd like to rest now,' and told me to do 'whatever it is mothers do'.

"Mister Frank hardly paid him any attention, and even Miss Millicent didn't do any of the usual things. Though she wasn't what you'd call a cold woman, she didn't feed the baby herself, I made up the formulas, and she seemed a little well, distracted."

Mrs. Sullivan was no gossip, but a kindly, warm-hearted Irish girl, nineteen back then. She became Mrs. much later. She didn't particularly enjoy talking about her time with Lennie's parents; nonetheless she obviously felt it was her duty to tell what she knew, and she'd always been surprised that so little had been made of the young couple's "strangeness", especially when Millie died.

In her view, it was Millie's mother who stepped in and made sure—"With money you can do anything"—that there was no real investigation when Millie died.

What did she make of it, then? Frank and Millie had an "affair" and only got married when Millie found out she was pregnant?

Henning thought that unlikely. If Lennie had been a love child, surely his parents would have lavished affection on him. It didn't sound like that. But was that the case?

"Certainly not. Leonard was a lonely child. Always off by himself."

"You must have had some thoughts about him, some conjecture," he said. "That perhaps Frank was not the father?"

She said: "I didn't like thinking that. It seemed disloyal, and Miss' Millicent was a good employer and showed me every sort of kindness. But I had to think that, didn't I? Mr. Frank didn't earn much. He was a decent and sensible man, but also a little cut off; they had no real friends, no one came to the house. Except Mr. Frank's mother, Mrs. Pimen. She married again when Mr. Frank's father died. I thought they were a lonely pair. It's possible, what you say. I don't know."

"Mrs. Pimen seems to have hated her daughter-in-law."

"I go see her from time to time. She's old and her mind's taken up, to be sure, with old grudges."

"She says Millie 'ruined' Frank's life."

"Maybe so. They weren't suited. But who can tell whose

fault that was, his or hers? They didn't 'connect', you know what I mean?"

"Mr. Frank would have known."

"Mr. Frank doesn't talk. The day after Miss' Millicent died, he told me I wouldn't be needed any more; he would look after Leonard himself. I said I would be happy to work out the period of my notice, the thirty days. He was very polite, but he said no. No explanation or anything, and I packed up my things and left. I was very sorry. I was the only attachment Leonard had."

"What sort of a child was he?"

"No trouble at all. Affectionate, quiet. He read a lot and played in his room. I took him to school when he started going, he brought his report cards back to me, not to his mother or father, and I had to pretend I hadn't seen them when I gave them to Miss' Millicent."

Henning didn't tell Mrs. Sullivan why he was asking about the family, and Mrs. Sullivan didn't ask. She didn't ask who he was or how he'd found her. When he got back to Sapphire, he said he thought the whole story had been a burden on her soul for many years, and that she welcomed putting her recollections in order.

Odder than that, however, was that she never asked what had become of Lennie, though she had been in all respects his real "mother" and she might well have thought Henning would know. In that respect, however, she was like almost everyone else: the family was one most people preferred not to talk about.

That anomaly apart, her plain straw hat, decorated with lop-sided flowers—brought out for many an Easter, and now specially, he guessed, for his visit—was proof of her honesty. Her account included nothing improbable or extravagant: it was a fair portrait of the secret complexity of families, of the secrets they keep.

She was a settled woman now; she liked regular developments, not sudden or surprising images; she wanted to be sure Henning understood before she came to that fatal Christmas Eve.

Normally, she said, she would have had the day itself off, and indeed she and her future husband's two sisters with whom she spent her Wednesday afternoons and every other Sunday, were putting up

Christmas decorations (which, she said decorously, were always put up "in the old country" on Christmas Eve, and taken down on the Epiphany) when Miss Millicent had informed her, on the eve—"At about nine o'clock," she specified—that Mr. Frank had been "called away". He was due back in time for the tree and presents and dinner: at the latest by twelve noon. Could she possibly come in just for the morning?

"Of course," I told her. She said, being a responsible woman, she could come right away if Miss' Millicent wanted. But Millie told her—in that "usual, rather cold voice she had, as though she'd thought long and hard about something and what she said reflected a firm decision taken"—that wouldn't be necessary. Leonard had gone up to bed, tired and excited, and she could manage perfectly well herself.

Plainly she had now arrived at the point in her story that was most painful. Henning could tell by the way she gathered herself together, wringing the little white gloves on her lap, adjusting her hat, putting in place a straggling curl, that she'd had trouble before getting past this point, Millie's death, that it cost her to *see it again*.

So there the two of them were, sitting in a proper parlor, tea brewing—two witnesses, no longer young, discussing things that had happened long ago. It was familiar to Henning from having happened often enough; and perhaps to her, too, having been, he thought, the subject of many conversations with herself.

It was a very cold morning—not of the sort that came with a dry high, even when the low sun failed to warm at all, but the kind of high-humidity, bitter cold that hovered in the teens and anticipated snow.

Mrs. Sullivan, with a scarf around her head and an old fur coat that Millie had given her the year before, in high boots and a wool dress ("I never have got used to wearing trousers and all"), left the warmth and friendliness of her future family's house, and walked over to her employer and her charge, the nine-year-old Leonard, a slight child with longish curly hair. She walked because she had never learned how to drive and, characteristically, she didn't want to bother anyone in the house to drive her over when they have so much to get ready.

She promised she would be back for Christmas dinner and managed a last smile for Henning as she explained how she always looked forward to the plum pudding soaked with good Irish whiskey.

The walk took her fifteen minutes or more, that being because, she explained carefully, as though she'd been derelict in her duties, there was packed snow and ice left over and "there aren't that many sidewalks when you get away from the main part of town."

Was that the house Henning had walked by, which seemed to him pretty small?

"Oh no!" she said, relieved to break off for a moment. "You mean the house where Mr. Frank lives now? No, it was a big house on the edge of town, a great big Victorian affair. It's been torn down since, it's where the elementary school is now, while the school Leonard was going to was behind the church."

She had her own keys, and she unlocked the front door, which was sticky, with as much care as possible, in case Millie were still asleep, who was often up late, reading, and "it wouldn't be unusual for Miss' Millicent to fall asleep again at around five or six."

She said the house was always overheated, and when she came in she always had to get out of her outdoor clothes fast, and take off her jumper if she had to clean. That was because the downstairs was full of big-leaved plants that required a lot of dusting, leaf by leaf. "It was a still house," she said. "And sad, too. It wasn't the sort of house where there was anything you looked forward to.

"Anyway, I struggled out of my coat and boots and put them up in the cupboard on the left as you went in. Then I thought as I was walking back to the kitchen through the dining room was that the mistress must be asleep, and perhaps the lad too. Since it was so quiet inside. I didn't think anything of it. It was almost always like that when I came down first thing, unless Mr. Frank was up and about. He *hated* the hothouse, and first chance he got he'd be outdoors for a long walk, no matter what the weather."

"What time was it?"

"About half nine," she said. Henning understood that for her there was a kind of relief in details, things that represented normality: where to hang a coat or put her boots. Millie's fussy side.

Weekdays, when Leonard had to go to school, Mrs. Sullivan got up at half past six; on weekends of holidays, breakfast would be at half past eight. If Leonard was up, he was supposed to stay in his room until she called him down for breakfast: "so as not to wake up his Mamma."

Mrs. Sullivan looked distracted. She knew that these details of routine were only postponing the inevitable, for suddenly, getting up energetically, and taking an album from a shelf under the TV, she said, "What a goose I am! And you probably don't know what Miss' Millicent looked like, nor the lad: shall I be showing you, then?"

Henning was startled at the few snapshots she'd stuck in her album. By herself leaving County Cork, a red-cheeked girl with wild, curly hair; then by Lennie, uncannily like a childish version of himself—except that his ears stuck out like two flaps of a cap; and finally by Millie, whom he had imagined as somewhat fey, perhaps pale, fretful or anxious, dark-eyed. Nothing of the sort. She was a solid woman, even buxom. She made a forceful impression, staring defiantly straight into the heart of the lens. She had masses of hair, but it was all bundled up and looked like it belonged (though she wasn't wearing the day the picture was taken) under a large felt hat with a bird attached to it with a heavy pin.

"That was only a month or two before…before she died."

"There are no pictures of Mr. Frank?"

"Oh no, he wouldn't allow that. Just like nobody could go into his room."

"They had separate bedrooms?"

"Surely. Always. Not even the boy was allowed in *there*."

"Was there something odd about it?"

"Nothing at all," Mrs. Sullivan replied. "Naturally I saw most of it at one time or another, when he was opening the door or shutting it behind him, or when the carpenter had to come to fix the sash on the window. An artist, Mr. Manning was. The carpenter. A fine strapping man with a good beard, brother to my own dear husband, Lord have mercy on his soul."

"So why was no one allowed in."

"I think it was a wee bit his museum like, you see. The furniture must have come from where he lived before they were married. It was a bachelor room."

"When did you first notice something was wrong in the house?"

"When I went up to Leonard's room. It wasn't right away, you know. I had to lay the table for breakfast—It was still all laid out when Mr., Frank came back, with milk in the jug, the toast in its rack as toast should be, the jams in a row—and then I had to clear up what Miss Millicent had left out for me from the night before, which wasn't much, she being forgetful about eating and meal-times and things of that sort."

Henning held the album on his lap. "She doesn't look like the forgetful sort," he said.

"Oh but she was. She could snap to suddenly and there'd be a list of things I hadn't done or Mr. Frank was supposed to do, and getting on after Leonard for not doing his homework. It's hard to explain, but it was like she'd be in the middle of that, all determined you know, and then, if she was driving a cart, and she let the reins slip from her hands and never thought about picking them up again."

"You went up to the boy's room?"

"He wasn't there."

"You went looking for him?"

"No, I knocked on Miss Millicent's door, it being a trifle open, thinking she might know, unlikely as that was!"

"And she wasn't there."

"The bed hadn't been slept in. Jesus, Mary, Joseph, I thought, where can she be? What can she be thinking of, leaving little Leonard alone? At that hour, if they'd gone out for some reason, surely I'd have seen them while I walked up?"

"You thought of the garden?"

"I knew Leonard liked to hide there, but I didn't think on a day like this. I did look out the back windows and there was no sign of them.

"No, worse than that was that her bed hadn't been slept in, and Leonard's bed had been slept in, his eiderdown up right by the head-board where it always was as if the poor child were hiding from the world. No, I tried the rest of the house first. Maybe they were playing tricks on me. But there was no sign of them, you see, and boys leave traces, even when they're hiding, things moved out of place. I went down to the cellar, I looked up the coal chute and the dumb-waiter, and at last I went up to the attic, which was full of things that Miss' Millicent brought with her and never used in the house, baskets of linen, stuffed animals her father shot…"

In the half-light of winter through the two skylights, iced over, and the feeble bulb at the head of the stairs, the worst thing for Mrs. Sullivan was—the first worst thing—was the normalcy of Millie in the middle of the room, staring right at her, though with her head at an awkward angle. Her comfortable body wore a white cotton shift and the pearls around her neck shone dully. Her hair was coiled up in braids on the crown of her head, perhaps as she'd worn her hair as a little girl.

She did not see, at first, either the rope that had been knotted over a great hook of the main beam, or that Millie's feet dangled a half-foot off the floor, her toes pointed up as though avoiding the dusty, dark boards and hampers alongside.

The second worst thing, far worse, was Leonard sitting on a little nursery chair that he must have removed from where his mother had knocked it over.

And worse than that, was Leonard's silence, and the way he stared at his mother, and the almost imperceptible swaying of her body, disturbed by the draft when Mrs. Sullivan had walked in.

"The silence," Mrs. Sullivan shuddered. "I was sent away by Mr. Frank, and I could never see Leonard again. Right after, I thought I might try and stop by to see the child, despite his father. But they left town soon after. I think they went to California. But I heard it was years before he said a word."

After, Henning was often to think that he never even wondered why Millie had taken her own life. It was as if irrelevant, and all that counted was Lennie doing his watching.

Chapter seventeen

Back in Sapphire, Henning, packing up his papers, went through the Xeroxed affidavits and depositions made in the early hours of their arrests. Dry-as-dust stuff by which horrible events are converted into legalese, which is free of pain and pretends impartial justice. "Comes now Detective Sergeant X..." The good Sergeant, "word for word under oath, doth state..." What the sergeant stated was terrifying enough, but his words and those taken from Lennie or Vance, from medical examiners, Sheriff Overmayer, Mary Kay, the customers of Hair Today, were *subsequent* statements. What had been done had been done and couldn't be undone. The truth was made to lie in the facts of the case, which were necessarily limited, which lacked the fullness and thickness of reality.

The testimonies established: Vance's purchase of specified sorts, widths and brands of duct tape and his going out for food half way through; Lennie's instructions and an inventory of his pharmacopoeia (its extent surprised the police, as did the absence of harder stuff); the time of the 911 call; the condition of various parts of Benji's body and its excreta (feces and vomit) and the provenance of the underwear stuffed in his mouth, not to mention vegetables (a single cuke, two carrots, a gnarled parsnip), nylon cord, a bandanna of Vance's, various belts, some webbing, a hypodermic and cotton balls from the salon downstairs.

They did not convey such intangibles as pain, fear or elapsed time, though Henning calculated it added up to some five-and-a-half hours, counting of course the amount of time it took Vance first, and then Lennie, to notice Benji was dead.

The affidavits described the victim, Benjamin Rapp, aged thirteen and eleven months, as lying face down on a bed: but not what kind of bed it was, or where placed, in what decor. Space, too, had become anonymous: the grievous, contended blank space between living and dying. Time had stopped or been arrested, compressed, at one specific point: "the time of death." Not how Benji *experienced* those hours, that time, whether it should last longer or pass more swiftly.

The documents also told Henning which cops arrived at the scene in answer to the 911 call, when, and some of what they saw, but not how they felt. Lennie made the 911 call, but the documents did not state in what circumstances, or why. Feeling what?

In his reconstruction, Henning started with the supposition that when the "boys" came back and sat around in the salon with so much time to spare in their world, upstairs, Benji was not inert, only befuddled by the pills which Vance had shoveled from his hand, jokingly, into his mouth. Not that he knew the hour of night it was when he came to—his pals had been away some hours—just that it was pitch black and that he felt sick. He needed to get to the bathroom.

First, he would have put his feet over the side of Vance's bed, which was also his from the time when he'd stopped sleeping on the back porch, and tested the familiar, cracked and curled-at-the-edges linoleum to see if he could stand up at all.

Feeling his way, he would, when he had got his bearings, have got up and sought the light-switch: only to find it didn't work. In passing, he would have felt the cold surface of the mirror at which he was accustomed to seeing Vance, at any time of day or night, studying his hair and then, his arm bent and held up level with his shoulder, giving his coif the few deft strokes needed to keep it in place.

It would have frightened him that he couldn't see himself, and would have been even more terrified if he could have seen what the affidavits said were strewn on the floor: his jeans, washed to an uniform light blue, and a mulberry-colored tee shirt with a round collar.

He felt himself naked, and was: but for the beaded Indian necklace around his neck which Vance had given him for his last birthday and of course the choker sliced from Captain Ron's bomber jacket.

It was likely that he gave some thought to what hour it might be (Vance's Rolex was their mutual time-keeper) and what was going on in the house.

It being Friday night, Vance might have come home drunk from the VFW and be sleeping it off down on the screened-in back porch. He would have wanted to know—because Lennie had turned into someone he no longer knew or understood— whether he was asleep in his room, which was just beyond the bathroom, or up, in which case he should move as silently as possible.

At best, if the lay of the land had been that neither Lennie nor Vance were there, or both were asleep, he might have been able to get to the bathroom, clear his head, and from there outside into the cool, clear air. Beyond that, so much being unknown, Henning doubted that he had any clear thought about what he would do next.

He probably would not have panicked until he tried the door to his room, started to turn the handle—probably thinking only that the bathroom was next door and he didn't have far to go—and found that even when he turned the handle all the way to the right (Henning had mastered all these details) and pushed the door with his foot, the door didn't budge.

Even then, chances were that he didn't panic.

His first thought would have been, since the door had *never* been locked before and, in fact, he had never seen a key for it—that the door had jammed.

Only after putting the whole weight of his slight body against the door several times would he have thrown off the poisonous fog in his head and become suddenly thirteen-year-old-aware: very sharp in the senses, very imaginative about danger, afraid of the unknown.

It could have been, since a great many possibilities must have suddenly presented themselves to him, that someone else had broken into the house and was standing, down below, waiting to hear if anything or anyone stirred. In Benji's place, Henning would have been as still as possible and sought to pick up the slightest sound or movement.

But these would have been unconscious thoughts, or subconscious thoughts. Akin to the bristling of hair on one's skin. Only after those inklings, similar to the floating world in which we pass from sleep to waking, would have something like "real" thought started. Given how Vance had been "training" him, he would by then have realized that the door was indeed locked.

The question was a simple but essential one: when did Benji cease to submit? Because struggle there had been, a desperate struggle. Much too late, of course: as the suicide, having leapt from on high, his arms flailing, might dream of reverse thrust.

That moment hadn't yet come.

Sensitive to every sound in the wooden house, Benji would have heard the front door of the salon open. Then Lennie and Vance talking. Not the words, but the tone of their voices. He would have strained to hear their words. They might be talking about him. That he couldn't make out. Lennie's voice would have been the one he used in business, matter-of-fact, perfectly controlled.

On the other hand, just then Vance sounded querulous, nervy, the way his mother was when Craig was about.

When Henning walked around the room that Benji and Vance had shared, the "crime scene," he tried both windows. Both gave onto the backyard and the roof of the porch, from which it would have been an easy drop for any agile boy. True, they had been covered and taped with black garbage liners. Still, nothing indicated that Benji had tried that way out, even for the sake of the light from outside, starlight and streetlight.

Henning took that to mean that the boy had not yet been desperate. If thoughts of escape had occurred to him, they might have been overlaid with the compliance he'd been taught, with the routine that had been established. That he was to be punished. And humiliated.

Supposing that Benji stood at the door, holding his breath, utterly still, he would have heard the tone of their voices shift down below. It was unusual enough for them to be talking in the salon, and not in the kitchen right underneath Benji's feet. Was it that they did not want him to hear what they were saying?

After what might have seemed a long time later, but was probably not long at all—certainly time was of no importance to Vance or Lennie, he would have heard Vance's steps on the stairs. Henning guessed that Benji would have got back into bed, which was where he was *supposed* to be. At the same time, it was unlikely that he welcomed those steps they way he once had. That could be deduced from Vance's testimony that when he unlocked the door and went in, Benji seemed to be still passed out from the pills Vance had given him. Benji was, therefore, conscious and pretending.

Here on the page was Vance shaking the boy gently by the shoulder and Benji turning over and looking up at him. (Vance was emphasizing his kindness and concern for the boy.) "He said he didn't feel so good, could he go to the bathroom?"

Ms. Baldwin, questioning Vance, asked: If they intended the boy no harm, why had they locked him in his room in the dark? Didn't they realize an adolescent boy might be terrified? Had they ever locked Benji in before?

Vance said no.

"Then why that night?" she asked.

He said: "Lennie said to."

Vance had taken Benji to the bathroom. The boy had been sick. He had retched for a long time. On his knees by the toilet bowl, his head half in.

If Lennie hadn't been coming up the stairs, Benji might have prevailed on Vance to let him go.

At least that was what Ms. Baldwin suggested in court. "The boy must have said something like 'I want to die'. That's what anybody would say who was that sick from what you'd been feeding him. You took him at his word? No, strike that, Your Honor. If he'd said, 'let me go,' would you have?"

"Conjecture!" Mr. Hoxey said.

All Vance said was that the boy stayed bent over the toilet bowl a long time, and Lennie was in the doorway looking impatient.

"Always your 'friend' Mr. Crace," said Ms. Baldwin. "Never you. But it was you who gave him more pills." She read from her police reports. "'Then Lennie said, "I'll give you something that'll make you feel a lot better."' Is that right?"

"I don't know about pills."

"You know enough to force them on a defenseless child."

The leather collar cut from Captain Ron's jacket was found behind the toilet brush in the corner. It had been torn off. If Benji had been struggling that would have happened when Vance yanked the boy's head back with one hand and put the other over his nose so he'd open his mouth and swallow the pills.

"You held him long enough so he had to swallow the pills?"

Vance replied, "Yes."

Ms. Baldwin said: "You did use violence, then. You forced him. Benji didn't want to."

"Lennie thought he was playing coy."

"Lennie again! If your partner was forcing you, you could have just pretended to give him the pills."

Vance said, "Lennie would have known."

Then Ms. Baldwin read out the pills listed in the autopsy. "I gather that amitryptiline takes a half-hour to an hour to work properly, and there's an "initial period"—I'm reading here—in which the patient, might as well call him the victim, could experience 'seizures, hallucinations, confusional states, disorientation, lack of coordination, ataxia, tremors, numbness, tingling and paresthesia of the extremities, abnormal involuntary movements, disturbed concentration, excitement, anxiety... In a thirteen-year-old?" Ms. Baldwin asked.

Vance said, "I told you, I don't know 'bout drugs. Lennie gave me stuff, too. I never asked."

"Why not?"

"Made me feel good."

"Did your partner use drugs, or did he just give them to you and to a thirteen-year-old?"

"Mostly Lennie did speed."

"Amphetamines."

"Yes Ma'am. Crystal."

The next last thing Benji would have seen in the bathroom before the drugs took over was Lennie standing in the door, unbuttoning his shirt, loosening the metal popper on the waist of his jeans, the neat line of hair rising to his navel. He couldn't have seen Vance, because Vance was behind him and bundling him from bathroom to bed, Benji's hands behind his back and soon tied with laundry line and then tape.

Some light must have come into Lennie's "darkroom", Benji's prison, Vance's bedroom, from the light in the bathroom. Enough, Henning thought, for Benji to realize he was entering the end game, that whatever was going to happen was going to happen *right then*.

Presumably that was when Benji had cried out. "No!" "Please!" Vance would have pushed him hard onto the bed? He hurt himself as he fell, his hands being tied behind his back?

As Ms. Baldwin coldly pointed out, "If the boy didn't resist and he thought this was just one of your games, why would you have been forced to gag him? If you hadn't, he might still be alive."

The last thing he would have seen was Vance stepping out of his pants and y-fronts. "Fruit of the Loom," said Ms. Baldwin, reading from the police report. "You took them off and stuffed them in the boy's mouth so he wouldn't yell, then you used exactly six feet five inches of tape wound round his neck to make sure it wouldn't come off."

In his head, Henning said: in spite of the darkness, the Kid would have been looking at Vance all that time, and that was something even Vance couldn't stand. For let's assume that in some part of his mind Vance genuinely loved the boy. But because of the look of reproach (fear?) Benji gave him, Vance took off the bandanna he wore about his neck and tied it over Benji's eyes. The boy would have been left with nothing but the smell of Vance's sweat, and Lennie's voice saying, "Turn him over. You better tie him down like it says."

There it was: Item Four on Lennie's list.

By then the pills must have been starting to work, because the boy was like dead weight when Vance lifted him up to turn him over, lifting his head off the pillow and—presumably answering a question from Lennie—saying, "Sure he can breathe."

What was next? Henning consulted Lennie's list. Next was tying his arms and legs at the corners of the bed: "Not so tight that he can't move. You'll need a little leeway."

Henning preferred to think that at this point, when he was being spread-eagled face down on the bottom sheet, Benji would have entered into a world of dream-like serenity as the pills took over. So that nothing that was happening—and certainly not Item Six, which consisted in lifting the boy up and putting a couple of pillows under his belly ("to produce the appropriate elevation for penetration")—was not happening to him, but to someone else.

Anticipation can be either pain or joy; one is wedged in the dentist's chair, tilted back, or one knows, from her warmth and smell and high humidity, that the woman is ready to receive. And sure, the anticipation can be more acute than what follows. However, the woman can be foresworn or postponed, the dentist by-passed. One has but to say no.

Benji had the anticipation but no liberty to alter his fate.

He could still hear, of course, but the sounds that reached him were confused, inconsistent, distant, and fluctuating. Two men moved about the room, Lennie less than Vance. Benji could sense their exertions. Once even certain drops of perspiration from Vance wet his lower back.

Which of them tore tape, unwound rope, unwound rolls of plastic? Helpless, how did Benji read what would happen next from what was happening now?

There would have come a moment, however, when for Benji the wait, the "before", was over. His body, especially its arched mid-section, swam in an unfamiliar sea. He bit on Vance's bandanna—a way of not floating. And when nothing happened for a few moments, he found he could not control the muscles in his body. It was simply too difficult to do. Or unnecessary to try.

His thoughts must have been as vague as his body. Where, in relation to him, was Vance, who was going to do the "doing" while Lennie watched?

Then as Vance positioned himself between Benji's legs, he would have heard Vance breathing, close enough for Benji to feel the warmth and moisture by his ear, and the scraping as Vance reached for the large jar of Vaseline that stood exactly where it had always stood, on the night table on Vance's side of the bed.

Hearing would then have given way to feeling: Vance leaning on the back of Benji's outstretched arm to reach the Vaseline; a single finger, two inserted and withdrawn; then Vance himself, collapsing on Benji's back afterwards.

At this point Ms. Baldwin had turned to the jury and said she would spare them the reading of the countless fantasies contained in Lennie's notebooks, "the dozens of things that *could* be done to a helpless child. I ask you to take my word that almost every one of them was done to the victim. Coldly, calmly, and without any trace of conscience."

He too would pass them over, Henning thought. The *manner* of insertion, *what* was inserted, were of secondary importance. What counted was that they gave pleasure and pain. No pleasure greater than the pain of humiliation, except of course the ultimate kick, which neither man had anticipated, which was death.

A couple of times Lennie called Vance back from his exertions. He said laconically, "Leave the cuke in there, but not more than a couple of inches. You could cause damage. Tape it so it stays in. So he *remembers*."

Vance said, "I'm hungry. You want something? I'll go over to the store."

"First you go do what I tell you."

Vance did, then took one of the pillows from under his belly and, puffing it up, put it under Benji's head, so he would be more comfortable. In court, Vance said he thought probably the Kid "didn't feel a thing," that he'd passed out.

"You went out and got some food," said Ms. Baldwin implacably. "And you wanted bananas."

"Yes Ma'am, I was hungry."

Henning had taken the same walk dozens of times. West two blocks to the Texaco station. It happened that the gas jockey on duty at three-fifteen that morning had played softball with Lennie. In court, he said Vance had been wearing a T-shirt on a cold night, and that he'd cleaned him out of his last packaged sandwiches. Two Camel filters. Bananas. Details. Of how rape makes you hungry?

Vance had left with his purchases in a plastic bag (found later), went a half-block and then came back. The store couldn't stock beer so he bought two bottles of Dr. Pepper. Rape also makes you thirsty.

"No ma'am," the clerk replied to Ms. Baldwin. "He didn't seem in a hurry or anything."

The State was able to produce both receipts from the Texaco cash register: the first for $6.47 and the second for $1.60.

The county coroner put the probable time of death between four-thirty and five that Saturday morning. Which more or less tallies with the time on the video in the Texaco store when Vance first walked in. The police found a Lennie notebook on the kitchen table. He was probably writing in it at about that time.

Vance came back and the two of them sat a half hour or so at the kitchen table. They ate the sandwiches and drank the Doctor Peppers.

Lennie said: "You think you can handle some more? You want some more pep pills?"

Vance said he wanted to go to sleep: "We're working later, right?"

So they called it a night. Except that Vance came out of his room saying the Kid had shat all over the bed. "Christ Jesus!" he said. "It's disgusting. The stench is something terrible."

Lennie said, "So clean it up. Open the window."

"I think I'll be sleeping on the porch."

Now comes the death, Henning thought.

While Vance went looking for a sleeping bag in the closet between the salon and the kitchen, or so he'd said to the police, he suddenly thought about Benji: "I mean, he deserved some sleep after all that." So he took a cutter from a kitchen drawer and went upstairs meaning to cut the boy loose.

First he ripped the blackout off the windows and opened them. After that he started cutting.

There was this about death, Henning thought, something that Vance hadn't imagined at all. That there would always be a struggle, however brief, however futile.

The Kid wasn't moving. His head was straight down and buried in the pillow. His neck, thick with fair hair, was rigid. There were bruises at his wrists from the rope. He resisted the terrible smell—the Kid had wet the bed too—and picked up Benji's head and moved it on its side. He yanked his y-fronts from Benji's mouth and started to undo the knot on his bandanna. "Lennie… Len-NIE!" He ran out of the room, gagging. "LENNIE! Get up here!"

When Lennie came up the stairs and walked into the room, Vance was shaking the boy, he was kissing him, blowing into him.

Lennie pushed him aside and did CPR on him.

"Lennie!" screamed Vance, in a voice tight with panic, "That's not how it's done. Let's call the cops—they know how to do CPR!"

Lennie was very calm when he went back downstairs and dialed 911. He said, "Yes, a kid. He was just staying with us and we were having some fun, playing games. Only he seems not to be breathing."

That was all he said when the cops came. That all they'd wanted was a little fun.

As always, however, when Henning came to this point, to the death of a child, to the violence used, up to and including death, against the very young—from one of his earliest compulsive descents into the dark side of life, the "execution" of a beautiful young girl like Emma H., to that of his own son, which occurred at the front door of his house, his home, and for which some had held Henning himself responsible—he simply could not go on. Each and every time he faced the events themselves it seemed they spoke for themselves and there was nothing for him to say.

About the author

Keith Botsford

H Magdalen (pronounced Maudlin) is the alter-ego used by Keith Botsford for what he, like Graham Greene, thinks of as 'entertainments'—stories of espionage and crime. Having been trained at law and once served in Counter-Intelligence, he has long specialized in crime stories in stints at *The Sunday Times*, *The Independent* and *la Stampa*. He says that he finds the strong narrative sense of crime stories refreshing. When he is not writing, he is a professor of journalism and history in Boston; and when not in Boston, is in Uzes in France. *Lennie & Vance & Benji* is the first of six stories featuring Henning Forsell, whose "business" is the history of crime, and whose passion is the motivation of ordinary people pushed to extremes.

*The fonts used in this book are from the
Garamond and Gill families*

II Magdalen's forthcoming book from Toby Press will be *Emma H*, the extraordinary story of a beautiful nineteen-year-old alleged collaborationist, 'executed' in Belgium in 1945.

Other works by II Magdalen are published by The Toby Press

Mothers by Keith Botsford (fiction)
Editors by Saul Bellow and Keith Botsford (anthology)
Sixth Form 1939 by Marcella Olschki, translated by Keith Botsford

TOBY CRIME
1. The Crime of Writing
2. Lennie & Vance & Benji

Available at fine bookstores everywhere. For more information,
please contact *The* Toby Press at www.tobypress.com